Gavin's MAGNIFICENT REVENGE

TAMIKA COLE

ACKNOWLEDGEMENTS

I give honor and glory to God who shows me daily, all things are possible through Him. Shouts to all the models I ever worked with. My characters were created from your image. Special thanks to my family and friends who always there for my complaining, but who's there to support and encourage me. Lastly, a big fat thank you to my only male model, Gavin A Wheeler. You represent my character well. God Bless you and your lovely family and God Bless my Readers!

CHAPTER 1

Quadir looked at his shirt, and when he saw the red dots lit up like a Christmas tree, he fell to the floor. His two bodyguards covered him as the bullet flew over Gavin's head. The targets were clear, and though Gavin was in the center of the shootout, the bullets met their intended marks. Bodies dropped from left to right, including Hakeem's. Bullets riddled his body as if he was target practice. He would require a closed casket due to the many shots he received. His hardcore life vanished in the blink of an eye. Quadir bodyguards got him safely out with only minor cuts and bruises. Once they got him to a secure location, he demanded that they round up his family.

"Man, what da fuck happened back there?" Quadir yelled when his bodyguards secured his location.

"I don't know, Qua. We definitely got caught off guard. Gavin musta had another team, but that shit won't happen again. I'll personally take him out," Shy one of his bodyguards replied. They messed up and Shy was hoping Quadir didn't turn on him.

"I pay you, bitches too much to have something like this happen! I lost all my lieutenants tonight—what the fuck!" Quadir said, shaking his head. He even felt bad for his most faithful servant, Hakeem. He never appreciated him when he was alive, and he knew it would be hard to replace his loyalty. This was horrible day for Quadir and he was out for blood. "I want his entire family dead!" he demanded. "Find out where his brothers are stationed, because this nigga needs to know everyone can be touched!" he barked.

"I'm on it, boss. I promise to handle this situation for you!" Shy assured, hoping he could redeem himself. The situation was embarrassing for him and his team.

"Yea, well you need to get back at me ASAP! I need to know who's protecting this wannabe Burger King! Get my family now!" he demanded and shy instructed his team to comply.

Meanwhile, Gavin was in and out of consciousness, but he could feel his body being transported. When they got him into the helicopter, he lost full consciousness again. And, just as Gavin had warned, the scene was gruesome and world news worthy with no witnesses or suspects. The handlers secured his family, but didn't give them any information regarding Gavin's whereabouts or even if he was still alive. They rounded up his family and took them to an undisclosed location. A month later, his family was notified.

When Ciani saw the news and the overturned SUV, she

panicked. For the past month, she was full of stress and the doctors had warned her to take it easy. Her blood pressure stayed abnormal, and the family was very concerned about her. Especially, Ms. Rhonda who wanted to be sure her grandchild would be healthy.

They didn't know where they were going, but once they were informed Gavin was waiting, it didn't matter. When they exited the plane, the huge Welcome to Mexico sign greeted them.

"Ciani, are you okay," Ms. Rhonda asked concerned for her and her unborn grandchild.

"The sun is making me feel slightly nauseous, and I haven't had morning sickness in a while," she replied.

"Well, hopefully there's some water in the limo," she said when the limousine pulled up. They didn't go through customs because none of them had passports and they were in Mexico illegally. The limousine driver drove directly off the tarmac and took them to their destination. Ciani realized they were in Cabo San Lucas by all the signs and the spectacular scenery. Momentarily, they all got lost in the beauty of the city, but when they pulled up to the magnif- icent villa estate, their mouths dropped. However, the armed guards positioned throughout the property and on the rooftop, intimidated them

When they entered the villa-like mansion, a slew of staff members greeted and led them to the wrap around terrace. The home was immaculate. It was perched on a cliff overlooking the marina with an unlimited view of the Pacific. They all took seats in the high end sleek gray lawn chairs and waited. Ciani was nervous and needed verification that Gavin was okay. When they realized they were being taken to him, they were willing to go to the ends of the earth. A few minutes later, their prayers had been granted when Annabella greeted them.

"Good evening everyone. I'm sorry you had to come all the way to Mexico, but we need you—Gavin needs you," She explained, and she had their full attention. Ciani remembered her when she came to the house and she was hiding in the hallway.

"I don't mean no disrespect, but when can we see Gavin?" Ciani asked.

"Yes, I need to see my son," Ms. Rhonda concurred.

"You're right, we won't keep you waiting any longer," Annabella replied. "I'm Annabella a business associate of Gavin's. I must warn you that your son is unresponsive. He's been in a coma for the past month, and it wasn't until yesterday that the doctors saw some normal movements. I thought this would be the perfect time to get his love ones involved," she explained.

"Ah coma, oh my God!" Ms. Rhonda cried. "Ciani, come here," she said when she saw Ciani break down. "You have to be strong for Gavin and the baby. Please calm down!" she pleaded.

"I can't, Ms. Rhonda!" she yelled as she bent over in

tears. "He's been in a coma for a month—what if he doesn't come out of it? And, why the hell are we just finding out?" she asked frantically.

"Take us to my brother!" Garin demanded.

Annabella led them to Gavin's room, but when they entered, Ms. Rhonda fainted when she saw him hooked to the tubes and ventilator machine. Garin and Kirk rushed to her aid, but Ciani was stiff as a board and couldn't move. She stared at her man, but he didn't look the same.

"What happened to my, baby," Ms. Rhonda insisted when she regained her senses. "Oh, my sweet boy," she continued in distress. Ciani's fear kept her from getting close. He had a bandage wrapped around his head and she could see the swelling from where she stood. He didn't resemble the strong reliable man she come to love. He looked shattered.

"Baby, we're here now, and we'll get you through this," Ms. Rhonda said trying to convince herself, as she stood by her son's bedside. "Allah will bring you through this baby. Nothing can stop the magnificent," she said with tears streaming down her face. She tried to be strong for the family, but she was deeply concerned about her son's future.

"Please, Annabella tell us what happened to him?" Ciani begged as she remained in her safe spot.

"Annabella, tried, but failed. Good effort though Anna," an unknown Mexican said when he walked into the room. "It's a good thing I was the plan B. I'm Salas and Gavin's been under my care for the past month. Unfortunately, he was kidnapped before I could intervene, and this is the results. He was brutally beaten and suffered a brain tumor. I have the best Neurologist money can buy and they removed the tumor successfully, but Gavin refuses to wake up. For the past week, he's been moving much more, which gave us hope. The neurologists suggested we bring you down to see if that would help," Salas explained.

"Let me explain a little further," Annabella interrupted, upset that Salas threw her under the bus. "The day Quadir kidnapped him, his goons beat Gavin nearly to death, and he was barely holding on when Salas reached him. We lost his trail shortly after he left the Summer Fest. I'll take full responsibility for this, but I truly did my best to protect your son. He insisted on going to that Summer Fest," she explained, trying to remove all the blame from herself.

"Brain tumor? Do you have *any* good news to share? I mean, so far this is just devastating?" Ciani said as she eased closer to Gavin. Her courage built as she realized her man needed her. She stood over his body and touched his swollen face. She bent down and kissed his forehead and told him she loved him.

"He's alive! He was on the ventilator for the first week, but he's breathing on his now," Salas explained. "Now that you're all here, I'm sure he'll come around. Please allow my staff to escort you to your rooms, and you can come back when you're settled. The nurses are here to bathe and check his vitals. Dinner is waiting, and my staff will cater to your every need. If you need me, just ask Annabella," Salas suggested.

They went along with the program and after dinner, they were all back in Gavin's room. Everyone was uneasy, but collectively decided to work together to help Gavin wake. Ms. Rhonda had come up with a schedule, so everyone could have his or her own personal time with him.

The following week, hope filled their hearts like the fresh ocean air they breathed. Gavin was making more movements and responding to his family voices, love, and prayers. The doctor's believed it was only a matter of time before he woke. Ciani barely left Gavin's bedside. She put aside her feelings and read the Holy Koran to him daily, praying it would help. And, she believed her prayers were being answered, because yesterday, she could have sworn she felt him slightly grip her hand. He was making movements that encouraged the doctors, but his post recovery was still in question.

"Hey, Doctor Vazquez. How's he doing?" Ciani asked when she walked into Gavin's bedroom. "I think we're close, Ciani. Whatever you're doing, keep doing that. I think he'll wake real soon. His vitals are all normal, but we won't know how he'll react to the brain tumor we removed. He may develop some cognitive deficits, but like I said, we won't know the impact until he wakes from this coma," he explained.

"That news is still promising, Doc. When he wakes up,

we'll cross that bridge then," she replied optimistic about his recovery. When the doctor left, Ciani returned to his bedside. The baby was kicking, so she placed Gavin's hand on her stomach, and the baby kicked up a storm as if he could sense his father's touch. "You feel that, Gavin? God gave that blessing to us. He's almost ready to meet his daddy, but we need you to wake up," she pleaded. Ciani was about to go empty her bladder, which seemed to be an hourly chore, when Gavin grabbed her hand, stopping her in her tracks. When she looked down on him, his eyes were closed. She needed to use the bathroom bad, but she was ready to piss where she stood after that incident.

"Don't go, babe," Gavin barely said.

"Gavin!" she screamed amazed. "Did you just say that?" she asked hoping she wasn't hearing things.

"Yes, babe," he whispered with his eyes still closed.

"Oh, Gavin! Thank you, God! Our prayers have been granted!" She raised her hands to the ceiling and praised God. "Let me get the doctor, sweetie, but I'll be right back!" she said and ran out the room screaming for everyone. Doctor Vasquez was the first to enter, and he examined Gavin.

"Mr. Douglas, can you hear me?" he asked.

"Yes," Gavin replied.

"Can you open your eyes, baby?" Ciani asked wanting to see his beautiful eyes.

"It may take some time for him to open his eyes. He

needs to get acquainted with his senses again," Dr. Vasquez explained.

"Gavin, momma is here, baby, and so is Garin and Kirk! We've been so worried about you!" Ms. Rhonda beamed when she reached his bedside.

"Yes, my son, we're all here and we ain't gon nowhere," Kirk his step-dad added. The road to recovery was uncertain, but they believed the worst was over.

CHAPTER 2

Gavin had made significant progress the past month. The only obstacle he endured was trying to walk. He never imagined struggling in the area until he tried. The doctors and everyone tried to warn him, but he was stubborn as a bull, and landed flat on his ass. The severity of his condition became clear and he was somewhat embarrassed. He requested Ciani stay away from that part of recovery.

However, his determination was admirable. Gavin recovered in less time than doctors predicted. Already, he was taking long walks down the beach and following orders. The doctor's said they could return to the states since his condition was stable and explained that Gavin would follow up with his cousin who had a practice in Delaware. Ciani was happy because she needed to follow up with her Obstetrician. Although, Salas provided one to monitor the baby and make sure Ciani was healthy, there was no place like home. Plus, she refused to let her baby be born in Mexico.

"Salas, my friend and the man that saved me, can we

talk?" Gavin asked when Salas walked into his gym where he was working out.

"What would ju like to know," he replied as he grabbed the fifty-pound weights off the floor.

"First, let me thank you, Salas. I don't know what the fuck happened, but I'm forever in your debt. What happened?" He asked dying to know how and why he saved his life.

"Ya gurl, Annabella, she's sweet, sexy, and smart, but you can neva trust a woman with your life, Papi. However, if I had to trust a woman, Annabella would fall in my top ten. Now, with that said, she lost you, but I find you. I know ju no killer, Gavin, and I know I put your back against di wall. I always like you, my friend and I couldn't stand back and let that peasant, Quadir win," he explained as he pumped the weights in his arms.

"So, you were watching me this whole time?" Gavin asked thankful.

"Always, Gavin. I've been watching, you and Quadir since you purchased your first kilo. I need to know what my money is doing, but here's the bad news—Quadir is still alive. This fuckin guy is lucky. But, here's the real deal, amigo... I'm getting out, so you'll have to handle that problem alone. I paid a hefty sum to break ties with di Cartel—half my fortune, my homes, and my many toys," he explained while Gavin listened intently.

"Get the fuck out of here!" Gavin replied in disbelief.

"No, get di fuck in here! I'm moving to the US to become

an Americano! And live life, my friend!" he answered as he did the Samba around the room. *What the fuck*, Gavin thought, but happy for Salas.

"What am I missing," Annabella said when she entered the gym. But before Gavin could greet her, she slipped into Salas arms and planted a sensual kiss on his lips. Gavin was sitting there like a deer in headlights.

"What da!" Gavin said, but pulled back as he watched the kiss build into a scene from an old-fashioned movie. "Hold up, what the hell is this?"

"This, my friend is di love of my life. She lights my fire, inflame my desiraaah, and burns my soul!" Salas responded and slapped Annabella on the ass.

"Burns your soul, nig? What's that supposed to mean?" Gavin asked fucking with Salas.

"We're engaged and we're getting married next week, Gavin. I know this comes as a surprise, but you can't help who you fall in love with," Annabella quickly replied.

"How did you two hookup?" Gavin asked entertained.

"After we lost you, I thought, Bill would kill me. I was looking over my shoulder twenty-four-seven. A week later, I received a call informing me you were alive and if I wanted to see you again, I needed to hop on a plane ASAP! When I arrived in Mexico, Salas was here to greet me, and he brought me to you. You can fill in the pieces on the rest," she explained.

"That's what's up, I was just surprised, but I'm happy

TAMIKA COLE

for y'all. I guess I missed a lot while I was sleep," he said, holding his dead down.

"Don't fret, Gavin. You have a second chance at life, so that's all that matters," Salas said, trying to encourage Gavin. He saw a change in Gavin and he was a bit concerned.

"Gavin, when you're up to it, we need to discuss the plan for when we get home," Annabelle said. "Right now, you're a missing and wanted person. You must turn yourself in, but it won't be for long, because when I release what I have, that whole precinct is going down."

"I have to go to jail—what the fuck?" Gavin replied agitated. He worked hard to stay from behind bars and now he would have to face something he never expected.

"You won't there for more than an hour. Trust me, they'll want to release you quickly! With that said, I told Bill that I can't protect you any longer—you don't listen!" she explained with a slight attitude. "He agrees because he lost trust in me which is understandable given the circumstances.

"Annabella, I never asked for this shit! You showed up at my house and pretty much took the fuck over, so don't come at me like that!" Gavin defended.

"Let's not argue amongst ourselves. Shit happens, and you take the good with the bad. I'm willing to lose half of everything I own for a peaceful life, my man! I say fuck, Quadir! Move to Beverly Hills and we can be neighbors si,"

"Nah, I ain't wit that shit, Salas! My people need me in the hood. Fuck I look like living in a big mansion when my

13

neighbors are struggling! Best wishes to you, but that's not for me.

"Have it your way, Gee! We wish you all the best too. Now, that we have that resolved, let's go join your family," Salas suggested.

Gavin spotted Ciani napping on the beach underneath a gazebo and decided to join her. *She's beautiful*, he thought as he admired her suntanned skin that glistened. Her belly protruded through the white sundress she wore. *She stuck by side*, he continued thinking to himself. His penis hardened, but he regained control, knowing they were out in the open. He was just getting back on his feet, so he didn't attack her vagina. But the war was on tonight.

"Hey, sexy wake up!" he whispered and kissed her neck. Ciani missed his touch and when she felt his breath on her neck, she woke up.

"Oh, Gavin, I missed you so much! I've been so worried not knowing if you were alive. When we saw the SUV turned over, and the news reported you weren't inside, I thought I'd die!" she said.

"I know, bae, and I'm sorry for making y'all worry about me, but I promise I'll never put you through that again. You're my world and I never want you to worry about anything. And, I'm sorry little man," he replied rubbing and speaking to her stomach.

"I know you've been working hard on making a full

recovery, but do you think you're ready to make love? I want to connect with you again, bae," she seductively pleaded.

"I thought you'd never ask," he replied and sensually kissed her. "Let's go back to the room!" he insisted.

They headed back to the mansion and Gavin couldn't get her to the room soon enough. She was slower than usual due to the load she was carrying, and he had to be patient. They passed his mom, sister, and stepfather in the massive media room and rushed to their suite. When they entered, he wasted no time on the love his life. He quickly lifted her sundress from her body and pulled her panties down to her ankles. She stepped out of them and he gently laid her on the bed. He dove into her moist garden headfirst and Ciani loved his tongue action. She was deprived for the past couple of months and the way he handled her clitoris was Heavenly. When he finished savoring her vagina, she returned the favor and sucked him raw.

"Aah shit, bae, do your thing," he said as he put the pillow under his head, so he could watch her grandness. He was on the brink of premature ejaculation, so he had to flip the script. He turned her over and entered her gently with a slight concern for his unborn child. He damn sure did not want to harm the baby or damage her vagina.

"Harder!" she demanded, and that was all he needed to hear. He slammed and hammered her sweetness until he couldn't take it no more. She felt so marvelous that he could not hold back any longer. "Damn, you're the shit, bae and the pussy is just as sweet as I remember it. Sorry, I couldn't hold out, but we can pick back up later," he suggested.

"Anytime, this belongs to you!" she replied, pointing to her wet vagina. "You can have it all!"

"That's right, love! That thing there belongs to me and me alone."

"I'm hungry, Gavin, and I don't think I can eat anymore Spanish rice. Can you see what's for dinner, babe? I've been craving steak and mashed potatoes."

"If my baby wants steak and mash, I'll make that happen," he replied. They showered together, and Gavin went to the kitchen to put in his woman's request.

An hour later, everyone gathered for dinner including Salas and Annabella. They laughed and enjoyed each other's company until Annabella summoned Gavin into Salas office. When he arrived, they were cuddling in Salas chair, and he was still trying to absorb that relationship. It was odd and unexpected.

"What are you two lovebirds up to?" Gavin asked, interrupting their crush fest.

"Loving each other!" Annabella stated with a huge smile. "Gavin, we need to talk about transitioning back home. Once we reach, the lawyers will be ready and waiting to escort you to jail! And, like I said, you shouldn't be held for more than an hour," she explained.

"A minute is too long, let alone an hour, Annabella, but I have no choice but to trust you!"

"That's all I ask for, Gavin," she replied.

"So, what's the plan?" he asked.

"It's simple, we go home, and everything will fall into place. Another thing, if I wasn't clear before, I can't protect you any longer. I spoke to, Bill, and he agrees that I should remove myself. Normally, I'd take that personal, but I have other interests outside of, Bill," she continued and looked at Salas.

"You gon just kick me to the curb—it's cool, I got that thick skin?" Gavin jokingly asked.

"That's good to hear, Amigo," Salas added. "Now, let's get a real drink."

Gavin and Salas enjoyed talking about the future together and Gavin was hoping everything worked out the way they wanted. And, in that instance, he thought about Quadir. He hadn't really given him much thought until then. However, his memory was full and unimpaired, and he remembered the torture well. He tried to block it out because every time he thought about it, it fueled his anger and he was out for blood. He knew exactly how to handle Quadir and relieved Annabelle was no longer a factor. Now, he could deal with Quadir on the streets. The next day, they all headed back home and landed at a private airport in Florida. Once they arrived, Annabella made sure their passports were available, and they caught a regular flight back to Philadelphia.

CHAPTER 3

*T*hey arrived at the safe house and Gavin attorneys were waiting. As soon as they saw them, everyone became tense. Ciani was hoping Annabella was right when she said they wouldn't hold him long. They only gave him enough time to shower and change. They advised the family to stay back for their safety. Although, Annabella was no longer protecting Gavin, he still had his security team that Bill provided.

"Gavin, remember, you'll only be in there for a short time. Get ready for fireworks!" Annabella boasted.

"I have no choice but to trust you, but can I ask you something before we go—how did you get a name like Annabella?" Gavin asked.

"My mother loved Italian names so, that's what happened," she replied.

"Okay, I'm ready. I love all y'all and I'll see you real soon," he replied and left. Ciani held back her tears until he was gone.

When he left, they all prayed and hoped for the best. Gavin had never been so nervous in his entire life. He wasn't no punk, but he feared confinement in any form. He worked hard to keep his business low key and off the map, but he allowed Quadir to disturb his success and livelihood. Now, he was turning himself in because of crooked cops. *This is some bullshit!* He thought when they arrived at the 5th District police station.

"Gavin, they'll ask why you didn't turn yourself in. Tell them somewhat of the truth. Let them know you were kidnapped, but the captures let you go after your family paid the ransom money. Explain that your family was scared to get the cops involved. They'll want the location of the drop off and where you were held. You don't know shit and they dropped you off on the street! You can pick a location," Todd, Gavin's lawyer instructed. He had a team of five attorneys walking him into the station. "By the time they blink, your investigation will be the least of their problems, and your family is being briefed as we speak."

"Don't worry, Gavin. This'll all be over before you know it," Annabella said, trying to encourage him. "Gavin, this is as far as go, but it was a pleasure working with you," she lied.

"Same here, and thanks for everything," Gavin replied, and his lawyers escorted him inside the station.

Annabella quickly reacted once Gavin was in custody. She called her reporter friend Brandon and told him it was time to release the tape she had given him a month ago. He was over the moon because he was itching to release it, but

Annabella made him promise to wait until she gave him the green light.

"Yes! I've been waiting, and I will make sure this hit the five o'clock news in fifteen minutes," he guaranteed.

"Great, I'll be watching. You can also report that Gavin Amin Douglas just turned himself in. I want the whole city to be aware of these crooked cops! The truth shall set him free!" she replied

"Once I release this tape, everyone will know. Agent Gray and the other DEA agents won't see this coming. He's been on the news hyping the situation up and honestly, it took a lot of restraint not to blast his crooked ass. We receive complaints about that district all the time," he explained.

"Okay, I'll let you do your thing, but I'm watching so get on this right away, Brandon," she warned. He owed her for saving his home from foreclosure last year. Annabella had many hats, and she was a financial adviser as well. When she hung up with Brandon, she called Bill. "Bill, Gavin is in police custody, but that shouldn't be for long," she explained.

"It better not be, Annabella! This has been daunting, and I haven't slept well in months. As soon as he's released, I need to see him! I'll have a private jet waiting," he instructed.

"Okay, boss, as soon as he's released!" she replied trying to reassure him that she had control. She knew he lost faith in her.

"Boss, I'm not your boss anymore, Anna. Did you forget

that quick, but thanks for everything you tried to do for my son? I expect there will be no more hiccups?" he asked.

"No more, Bill! I'll bring him to you as soon as he's released!" she quickly responded and ended the call. She was embarrassed that she allowed Gavin to slip through her fingers.

The five o'clock news began, and Annabella was champing at the bit. She called Gavin's family and told them to tune in. As soon as the news began, it led off with Gavin's story and the video with Agent Gray and his team. Breaking News flashed across the screen and she wished she had some popcorn.

Let's dive right in! We have breaking news that you will only see on this network! You may remember a couple of months ago, the police issued an arrest warrant for, Gavin Amin Douglas also known as, Gavin the Magnificent! He was wanted in connection with drugs discovered at his Tow Truck business. The video we're about to show is disturbing, folks!

After the video played, Gavin received his justice. The entire city had access to crooked Agent Gray and his fellow police goons. Annabella was pleased with herself. The tape had sound, and the city could see and hear Agent Gray plant the drugs and discover them at the same time. This looked bad for the PPD, but it was vindication for Gavin and Annabella. She failed Bill and hoped this made them square. The news reporter explained that they reached out to the

PPD and the commissioner, but they had no comment. Bill called Annabella back and reassured that she redeemed herself. That placed a smile on her face, and though she had new a venture with her fiancé, she never wanted to leave an employer on bad terms.

*M*eanwhile, over at the police station, Gavin attorneys were going ballistic, demanding that they release him immediately. This was a huge embarrassment for the PPD. They all scrambled around trying to make sense out of what they just saw.

"You will release my client now!" Brandon barked. He was the lead lawyer, and he was a savage. "We'll be filing a major lawsuit against the city, and I plan on taking this entire station down! I won't ask again!" he demanded.

It took them another hour to release Gavin after the Sargent reviewed the tape. This looked horrible for their precinct and he had no choice but to let him go and drop all charges. When Gavin was booked, the detectives tried to intimidate him by using scare tactics. However, this may have worked on someone who was guilty, but Gavin knew they didn't have anything other than the drugs they planted at his business. He remained silent during their aggressive interrogation, which pissed the detectives off further. As he walked out the police station, he had the last laugh and you could see the embarrassment coming from their faces. He had his dream team by his side, and happy he could bury that chapter of his life.

"There's a private jet waiting to take you to Miami. Bill is demanding to see you today," Brandon explained.

"Today, I was hoping to just go home," Gavin replied.

"I'm just your lawyer and the messenger. The rest is up to you, but your transportation is right over there," Brandon explained, pointing to the Bentley across the street. *Bill is always extra*, Gavin thought before parting ways with his attorneys.

Gavin was feeling slightly weak when he boarded the plane, but he was happy to see a nurse and doctor aboard the flight. As soon as he took his seat, they checked his vitals and gave the pilot the go. Gavin called his family to let them know what was going on because he didn't want to worry any more than they already had.

Over at City Hall Councilman Dave Chapman was disheveled after watching the spectacle on tv. He was nervous that Agent Gray would cooperate, and out him and the other council members. He wasn't prepared or willing to lose his job and possibly face prison time. He needed to cover his tracks and get rid of Agent Gray. He could not afford for any negative publicity to fall in his laps. He called an emergency meeting but left Councilwoman Tamika Butler out the loop. As far as he knew, she didn't know how much he was involved and he wanted to keep it that way. The only members in attendance were himself, Representatives Lynwood Rogers and Earl Waterfield. They met and plotted on ways of protecting their part in the corruption. However, Councilwoman Tamika had done her own dirty work. She planted a baby monitor inside of one his plants by the window, and she was stunned to hear their plan. Councilman Chapman had no intentions on letting Gavin off the hook. He vowed to bring him down by any means necessary. She needed to warn Gavin. She had no plans of running for a second term once she found out how crooked and vile the system was. She realized she would be more affective on her own.

CHAPTER 4

Quadir was fuming. "You see this fuckin shit!" Quadir spat when he saw the news. "This little bitch must have nine lives or some shit! Now they release this nut. You know what, I'm glad he's out, because I can finish what Hakeem started, maybe he'll rest in peace then!" He continued as he talked to Bones another one of his new lieutenants.

"Yo that nigga lucky ass shit, but everyone lucks run out at some point!" Bones replied ready to get at Gavin. He needed to prove himself worthy of his new position and he was ready to take Gavin out.

"I won't be able to sleep until I know this nigga is six feet under! Do we have anything on his whereabouts, and what's up with his family?" Quadir asked.

"No news yet, but wherever he's holding his family, must be in a secure location, because we have nada. His brothers came home, but one is back for good. I got a friend serving in the Army and he told me his youngest brother Gerald, ain't reenlisting, so we should be able to get at him soon," Shy explained.

"That's good news! Until we can get his ass, we'll take his family out! I want him to feel my fury! I hear he's about to be a father. If you can get custody of his lady, I'll forever be in your debt," Quadir said encouraging Bones. "Fuck, Gavin for right now! What the fuck is up wit my money?"

"We good, it's as if nothing has changed! We're all sorry for losing Hakeem, but the team is still winning. Matter fact, we're bringing in more money! I have some new recruits coming in tomorrow for you to feel them out. And, I want to thank you for the promotion and the trust," Shy replied.

"Don't think me yet, Shy. I never said I trusted you. This is a trial run, my nigga, so don't fuck it up!" Quadir warned.

"I feel you, but I'll prove myself," he replied.

"No doubt. But what I need from you right now— is a secure location for my wives! This living in the same household ain't working and they bout to kill each other! I need peace and they need their own shit!"

"I'm on it. I should have something lined up by the end of the week," Shy reassured.

"Yea and make sure Gavin is dead by the end of the week too!" Quadir advised and dismissed him.

When Gavin arrived at Bill's condo in Miami, you would've thought it was his birthday. Bill had orchestra an entire *Glad Your Alive* celebration. Gavin didn't know what was going on, but when he looked across the room and saw his family, including his brothers, his heart was lifted. He wanted to rush over and greet his family, but Bill was anxious to show Gavin some needed attention.

"Son, I can't tell you how happy I am to see you! You had us all scared, but I went deep and prayed," he said as if he never prayed before. Gavin was slightly baffled, but he allowed that to go over his head.

"I'm blessed to have a friend like you, Bill! You're a great father figure and you've done a lot for me, my career, and my fam. I'm forever indebted!" Gavin replied meaning every word. He finally understood how much Bill cared about him, the man, opposed to their business relationship.

"That's means a lot, dog. Now go enjoy the party. We can chat later," he said, trying to be cool.

"Aight, my dog later!" Gavin laughed and walked away. He hurried towards his family, and his youngest brother Gerald was the first to hug Gavin.

"Brah, when I heard the shit that went down, I didn't reenlist! Fuck the Army and fuck Quadir!" Gerald whispered.

"Yo, B-Smoove, you need to chill little brother!" Gavin replied, calling him by his hood given name, because he was smooth with the ladies. "I don't want you getting involved with this shit. I'm not mad you quitting the Army, but I can use you in a more productive way. I need someone to run my restaurants—all of them so, you won't have time for this game!" Gavin suggested.

"I can do that, but it's too late for turning the other cheek—sorry," B-smooth replied with a dumb expression.

"We'll discuss this later," he said and embraced his oldest brother Greg. Greg was devoted to the military and everyone knew it. Gavin didn't have to worry about him trying to get revenge. However, his younger brother was a hot head and always problematic. He shocked the family when he enlisted and made it past training because he wasn't known for taking discipline well.

"Gavin, what the fuck, man?" Greg asked confused. As far as he knew his brother was the pride and joy of the family. "Come here, man. I'm happy your alive bro," he hugged him tight but quick. Greg was trained to keep his emotions in check and he sought of broke the rules.

"I appreciate it, but I'm good and trust me, I won't be caught slipping again!" Gavin reassured.

"I'm glad to hear it. So, this is how the rich folk get down, huh!" Greg replied, changing the subject and they both laughed.

"Yea, this how they do. I'll be right back, Greg. I need to check on Ciani." Gavin noticed she didn't look that well, and he wanted to make sure everything was okay. "Baby, you feel okay?"

"Now that you're by my side, I do! I'm just giving you time to adjust to our life again. I hope I'm a part of your future?" she asked nervously. She noticed a change in him since he woke up even if no one else had.

"Where is this coming from, Cee? You, you're the love of my life. You complete me and without you, there is no me, babe. You don't know that?" he asked confused at her insecurity.

"Yes, I know that," she quickly replied pacifying him.

"Don't ever forget it and when this party is over, I need you to pick a date," he said leaving the last part open.

"Ah date? You mean for the baby shower?"

"Nah, I mean for you to become my wife and lifetime partner. I've been giving this a lot of thought. We can have a small ceremony—you, me and the Iman. I'm willing to accept your Christianity on one condition."

"And, what's that?" she asked slightly agitated.

"We have to be married by the Iman and it'll be just me, you, and God. That's all that really matters. We can plan something for the family afterwards. What do you say, babe—you wit that?"

Fuck no, she wanted to say. "Okay, Gavin but you have to promise to get the marriage license," she agreed.

"Great, sweetheart!" he replied, thinking that went much better than he had expected. "Once we get through all of this, I'm taking you away on a vacation. You deserve to see the world, Cee, and we'll explore it together—you have my word."

"I'll hold to you to that, handsome." Everyone enjoyed the party, and Gavin was happy and satisfied. His brother

Greg had to leave but Gavin was happy he took time from his busy schedule.

"Gavin before you leave we need to talk," Bill said.

"Okay, let me holla at my fam real quick and then I'm all yours," he replied. A few minutes later, he and Bill went into his office.

"Gavin, I need you to stay alive. This whole Quadir thing needs to be a thing of your past. I think you should consider relocating. There are so many beautiful places in the country to live—why stay in Philadelphia?" Bill asked concerned.

"If I didn't know any better, I'd say your dissing my city. It's like this, that's my heart and soul! This lifestyle attracted me, but it never resonated well because I don't desire this shit—I'm just a rich city boy trying to make a difference!"

"I didn't mean no disrespect towards your city. I'm just saying, Gavin, you can do good and help your people living in any city!"

"I feel you, but there's nothing like being in it and knowing where the most help is needed. Listen, this isn't up for negotiation. I don't plan on living in the city, but I plan on being in the city, daily. The youth in my city is fucked, and all the soda and cigarette taxes ain't solving shit!"

"You figured out the problem?"

"Yea—hope, there is none and I need to try to restore that sentiment!"

"I guess I'll have to beef up the security then?"

"Nah, Bill. I just need them to protect my family, but pull the plug on my security. I need to handle my existing problem the way I know best," Gavin said, already knowing how he would handle Quadir and his goons.

"Are you sure? I don't think I'm comfortable with that," Bill protested.

"I'm sure and I mean that shit too!" Gavin insisted "Just make sure my money is right. You know I'm down with on the business end because I'll need to put that money back into my community. Next year, I plan on changing lives like nothing the city has ever seen before."

"I see I have no say in the matter!" he replied disappointed. "I'll grant your wishes and give you this check I've been holding for two months," Bill replied and handed him the check. When Gavin saw the amount, his knees buckled.

"Fifty million, Bill?"

"That's your cut from the pipeline not to mention the residual monthly income that'll be coming in. Stick with me, kid and I'll make sure you have enough money to fund your projects!"

"You ain't never lied!" Gavin said enthusiastically.

They concluded and resumed to the living room where his family was waiting. He was itching to get Ciani back to the hotel. Bill rented an entire floor at the Four Season's and he wanted to bond with his love and his new bundle of joy. He gathered his family, and they all went to the hotel. Gavin devoured and invaded her body with love, passion, and extreme gratitude. Ciani had never felt more loved nor had she ever experienced an orgasm like the one he provided. He showered her with love, the type of love us ladies thrive on. He bathed her and rubbed her down with her favorite body butter by *Josie Maran*. He sang to her and the baby which only increased her love for him. Though, he could use a few singing lessons, she knew he was sincere and extremely comfortable with her. They had no secrets and no bad blood between each other, but Ciani noticed a change. She couldn't put her finger on it because for the most part, he was acting the same. But, she knew something was slightly different. She brushed those feelings under the rug, because that night, she was floating in his love.

Down the hall in Ms. Rhonda and Kirk's room, another sexual encounter was taking place. Ms. Rhonda finally had Kirk where she wanted him. He couldn't hide downstairs on the couch that night. She brought along his Viagra so there was no excuse. She thought when Gavin moved they would get their groove back, but Kirk was turning into his old boring self again. She hated that she had to sneak and put a little Viagra sprinkles in his food, but she was running out of options. A non-working dead dick was not part of the plan. However, Kirk was in a romantic mood, so he willingly took the pills. Ms. Rhonda was in Heaven because he received the full dose and performed a hundred percent better. She realized the few shavings wasn't potent enough.

Garin had broken up with her boyfriend because of his stank feet, but she missed him something awful. He tied her hands when he refused to seek help. She butchered his pride and after a heated argument, he packed up and left. His sister Kira told her he went to the doctor's last week. Garin became hopeful until she said his feet still smelled like the dead, and his mother forced him into the unfinished basement. Garin knew she had to get over him and his long penis.

Greg was in his suite focused on getting back to work. He loved serving in the military and that's why he wasn't in a rush to get married. He lived and breathed his job and there wasn't much room for anything else besides family. He went to bed dreaming about getting back to the base.

B-smooth was angry and plotting on ways to kill Quadir. He idolized Gavin and when he heard what went down, he knew he made the right decision to quit the Army. His brother needed him, and he would kill Quadir and avenge his brother.

CHAPTER 5

Quadir's drug business was up and running. He hired a slew of foot solder's and promoted some to lieutenants. He found a new, undisclosed location to have his monthly meetings. However, this meeting was unlike any he had ever held before, because he was about to send out a hit that would shatter Gavin's world. He was tired of playing games with this fool. He missed out on a lot of money and he planned to unleash his poison back into the community where it belonged.

"Your new soldiers are waiting for you. You ready to meet your new team?" Shy asked.

"No time like the presence," he replied, and they left. "What's up lil nigga's? Y'all ready to get this money?" he boasted, and they all yelled yes. "First, I'd like to welcome you to the team, but there are a few things we need to discuss," he explained.

"I'm ready to do whatever you need!" One of his new worker's yelled

"Good, good—what's your name youngin?"

"Abelon, but everyone calls me Abe," he replied.

"Welcome, Abe and thanks for confirming your loyalty. See loyalty is key in this business and y'all still need to prove yourself! I don't trust a fucking soul, and with that said, this envelope contains contact information about your family! Their lives are in your hands, because if any of you ever cross me, I'm taking it out on your entire family!" he threatened, but they already knew he was psychotic. "I have another problem up for elimination. I know you all heard of that punk ass nigga, Gavin the Magnificent! Well, I need him and his entire family dead! Whoever is the first to bring in dead Douglas's will be promoted to Lieutenant and gain my trust!" he encouraged.

"I can help you out there!" Abe quickly responded. "My sister is friends with Garin and they talk often. I'm sure I could get her address," he said confident.

"Yea, you do that! And, that goes for the rest of you muhfucker's! You'll be paired up with one of my journeymen until you get the hang of shit. Now, get the fuck out!" he barked and left the room.

When he arrived at his temporary home in Glenolden, Pa, fifteen minutes away from Philly, he felt the tension between Mahassin and Kim as soon as he walked inside the house. Being greeted with two angry women when all he wanted was peace, was frustrating. Kim was the true problem because Mahassin would do whatever he wanted.

"How are my two favorite women doing?" he asked already knowing the answer.

"This shit ain't gon work out, Qua! I mean—I can deal with a lot of shit, but this is too much! I'm ready to cut my own throat," Kim spat.

"Help yourself!" Quadir replied, tired of her complaining. She sucked her teeth and stormed away. "Kim!" he yelled. "Bring your ass back here!" She reluctantly stopped in her tracks and obeyed. "You know we all eat dinner together, so stop acting like a spoiled brat!"

"I'm not hungry," she sighed and sat at the dinner table ready to cry a river. However, she would never give him the satisfaction, so she sucked up those tears. That was a better look for weak ass, Mahassin the Maid.

"I don't give a fuck! Just sit there and look pretty like you always do!" he countered. "Baby, what you cook?" he asked Mahassin.

"Steak, I thought my king deserved a piece of my delicious ribeye. I have baked potatoes and corn on the cob too! Outback ain't got nothing on your girl," she boasted.

"I know that's right, babe! It smells good—I can't wait to taste it!" he responded, knowing Kim hated every minute. He didn't care either way. It was Kim's night, and she was coming off that pussy regardless of her mood.

Kim wanted to vomit, and she was so disappointed in herself and her life choices. She knew she could no longer play Quadir's game, and she was planning her escape. She had stashed away a good some of money from her salon and the money Quadir gave her the past two years. The thought of starting over in a new city was encouraging, and she was gravitating towards Atlanta. However, she knew the hair competition would be fierce, and she wanted a straight man. Atlanta wasn't known for that, so she decided she would move to California. It was across the country and she always dreamt of living in a warm climate. With this new threat on the family life, her plan would have to wait a while longer. She legally changed her name three months ago, and now she just needed to find the perfect escape.

*T*he first thing Gavin did when he reached his safe house was to check on his businesses. His managers gave him the status and things weren't as bad as he expected. Since his mom, sister, and Ciani were no longer handling his business affairs, some things got out of control. His daycares needed his mom, but he couldn't jeopardize their lives. Much to his regret, he shut down Gavin Magnificent headquarters. He planned to open another one at a new location with a new name. He learned the hard way the art of discreetness and he would never risk his family or employees again. He felt good to have his little brother back, but he knew B-Smoove was hot headed and that worried him.

"Yo, Gee, where am I sleeping?" B-Smoove asked when he walked into the kitchen where Gavin was at.

"All the rooms are taken, but there's a pullout sofa in the

basement. It's finished and there's a TV and surround sound down there.

"That's cool with me since I don't have no other choice."

While everyone was happy to have Gavin back, B-Smoove was plotting on revenge. Unbeknownst to Gavin, he contacted his friends at the bike club and got them onboard. They planned a surprise welcome home party, and he needed to get Gavin to that party. He knew it wouldn't be easy with all the family crowding him, but he had to try.

"Gee, I spoke to the Savages, and they planned this party for you. It was supposed to be a surprise, but it's going down tonight. What's up you down or what?" B-Smoove asked.

"Damn, I don't think I can make that. I've been trying to chill and spend some quality time with the fam especially, Cee," Gavin replied.

"Aight, I'll call them back and tell them you can't make it," he said disappointed.

"Hold on, let me see what I can do," he responded, because he could use the distraction and he hadn't seen his crew since the Summer Fest.

"Yea, go get that approval from, Cee, because I see she's running shit!" B-Smoove teased.

"Shut the fuck up, man! I'll be right back." He left the basement hoping Ciani wouldn't give him a hard time. When he entered the bedroom, Ciani was in a deep sleep. He noticed she slept often, but he figured the pregnancy was taking its toll. "Baby, wake up," he said, and she woke up rubbing her eyes and stretching her arms.

"What's up, my king!" she replied and gave him her full attention.

"I was hoping you wouldn't mind if I went to the bike club tonight. They planned this big celebration for me and I would hate to disappoint them. Plus, I haven't seen them in a minute," he rationed.

"Gavin, we just got back. Can't it wait a little?" she asked yawning.

"I know, Cee but I promise to be careful. I'll even take security with me and I'll be back before you know it," he said, trying to convince her.

"Gavin, one thing is for sure—I cannot stop you from doing what you want. I don't want to be overprotective, but I rather you stay home. However, with all you've been through you deserve to enjoy life, babe. Call me when you get there, and you better not forget," she said appeasing him. That small gesture of her allowing him to be the man was why he loved her. Outside of converting to Islam, she was always flexible with his wishes.

"Thanks, bae. I'll call you as soon as I get there!" he said and rushed away.

Gavin and B-Smoove headed over to the bike club with security following. When they reached the club, Gavin could hear the music and fun from the outside. He couldn't remember being so excited to see his friends and just have some him time. When they entered the club, everyone stopped what they were doing and embraced him. He felt loved and respected.

"Welcome back from the dead, big head! We were all worried to death!" Patches greeted with her beautiful fat ass. She was sexy as shit and any of the Savages would've wifed her, but she preferred women. She was a thoroughbred, pretty in the face and fat in ass.

"Thanks, sweetheart! I really appreciate the love," he replied and hugged her. She was so soft, and she smelled good which gave Gavin an instant hard on. He regained his senses, remembering his true queen was home waiting.

"Mag, welcome home, but what the fuck happened?" Peanut asked. "I mean the last time we saw you was at the Summer Fest and then later that night, we see on the news that your truck was overturned, but you were MIA nigga!"

"I know right, that was some bullshit, but you know they can't keep the Magnificent down! Listen, Peanut, we can get into all the details later. I just came to enjoy myself and show my appreciation," Gavin replied.

"I feel you. Help yourself to the food and drinks. This shit is all for you, brah!"

"Yea, we bout to get turnt da fuck up!" Flex another biker said.

"You've been missed, brother!" Pop added. "We need to

talk before you leave. I know you tried to keep us out the drama, but this shit affects us all. Word on the street is that Quadir put a hit on your entire family! I don't mean to bring you down, but the Savages are ready to play—if you know what I mean. Go and enjoy the festivities, but after you catch up, we need to have a sit down," Pop explained ready to war for Gavin. Plus, they just received confirmation that Quadir was responsible for killing his cousin last month.

"I got you," Gavin replied and mingled with his crew. He was in his element and he felt like he was around family.

"B-Smoove, when they let you out?" Peanut asked.

"Nigga, you act like I was locked away in jail. But to answer your question—a few days ago," B-Smoove replied inhaling the smoke from the blunt he had. "I ain't have weed in years," he coughed. "This shit is the bomb."

"No smoking in the club, Bee! You need to take that out back!" Pop said when he smelled the sweet-smelling herb. He didn't indulge in drugs, but he didn't judge people who smoked marijuana. However, he wasn't having that shit in the club. Since Gavin was MIA, he took over the duties as President, but he was willing and ready to relinquish that authority. Everyone enjoyed themselves and before they knew it, more ladies had arrived, and all the attention was on Gavin. He basked in all the care and affection they showed, and he was feeling like the old Gavin again. He laughed, flirted, and behaved slightly devilish towards the women unable to help himself. He couldn't help but feel up a few asses and allow them to rub their breast against his chest. As the night calmed, he was ready to leave before shit got of hand.

"Pop, I'm about to head out, but I know you wanted to talk. You think you can make that happen quickly?" Gavin asked ready to get home. He needed to feel and touch Ciani and the baby. "Pus, I don't know how long I can control Jeffries!" he said grabbing his penis. I'm tryna be good to my good woman!"

"I feel you. We were all waiting on you. Let me round up everybody," Pop said and left to gather the crew.

"Brah, I don't what the fuck you got yourself into when I left, but if what I'm hearing is true, it's time for Quadir to go to sleep permanently!" B-Smoove said, leading off the conversation once they settled into one of the private rooms inside the club.

"What the fuck is you talkin bout, Bee? Yo, you ain't getting involved in this shit! I don't know what's been going on in that wondrous brain of yours, and I can only imagine— but hell no!" Gavin spats. "Man, I'm bout to fuck you up! Is this what this party is about?" Gavin asked pissed and confused. He didn't want his friends involved with Quadir shit. He planned on pulling in a few friends who he knew could handle the situation, but he wasn't feeling them.

"You can't stop that, Gavin! This nigga tortured and turned you into a fuckin vegetable, Gee? Nah, like I said

42

before, night-night nigga!" B-Smoove replied sticking to his guns.

"Yea, Mag, I'm wit, Bee on this shit. This nigga thinks he some sought of God! I ain't gon lie though, he got the entire city on lock pushing that weight!" Sharif another biker added. He came to play, but only if they had a solid plan. He wasn't about to risk or lose his life for Gavin, but he was down for cleaning up the streets anyway necessary for the safety of his family.

"What the hell y'all got planned, because it's obvious I'm the only one in the dark?" Gavin asked.

"I can speak for myself and say I want this pussy dead! His time of terrorizing the streets of Philly is, over! It's gonna get ugly because we bout to go to war!" Pop added. "I got my peeps ready to put in some work!"

"I got like twenty men," Bishop chimed in. "They're locked, loaded, willing and ready. Quadir affected all the lives of my crew so, they ready to put an end to him!"

"See, Gee, we got this," B-Smoove added, and happy Gavin was coming around.

"I guess y'all got this all figured out, but you all missed the point. I'm not trying to go on no killing spree to take down our own—our youth," Gavin rationed. His brother and friends were ready to get Quadir and all his little ducklings.

"Man, I feel you, but fuck that! Those little thugs wouldn't hesitate to take any one of our lives! They don't give a fuck about themselves so, you know they could give two fucks about us! What you want us to do—ask if they'll be good and stop killing the innocent? I don't think so, Mag. We need to go in guns blazing, nigga! We have to speak their language!" Pop countered.

"Yea, Gee, these punk asses don't give a fuck! Quadir MO is placing fear and order into their minds. It's as if they get brainwashed," Bishop concurred. He was the oldest of the bunch nearing fifty, but he was ready to ride with the Savages on this issue. Philadelphia was one of the biggest crime cities in the United States and the killing wasn't slowing down.

"We need to be smart about this shit! Like I said, I'm not a hundred percent with the killing, but I understand. After y'all round up your crew, let's revisit this conversation. For now, I need to get home to my pregnant lady." He told his brother he was ready, and they left after Gavin said his goodbyes.

Quadir was pissed when Kim came home. "Kim, where da fuck you been?" Quadir spats and smacked her hard across her face. He was tired of her disrespectful self and he gave specific instruction she wasn't to leave the house without him knowing.

"Why the fuck you hit me!" Kim yelled. That was the last straw and as soon as she found a way to escape, she was bouncing. "I had a gynecology appointment because my pussy was itching! When you have sex with multiple women without protection, it fucks up my PH balance! I have a bacterial infection," she continued as she held her face. "See!" she said handing him the prescription for the cream she was given. "I think Mahassin needs to take her ass for a visit. I'm sure she has the same shit!" She stormed off and went to her room to pray. However, she chose to pray to God through Jesus. She needed him to save her from Quadir's evil ass.

After looking at the prescription, he felt slightly bad for smacking the shit out of her. However, she was problematic, and he had no more tolerance for her minor complaints. He knew she didn't love him, but he also knew she wasn't going nowhere. In his mind, she was his forever. He went into the kitchen and his loving wife Mahassin was cooking. He could always depend on Mahassin and he made a note to himself to treat her to something special.

"Hey, babe, how was your day?" he asked and Mahassin was pleased he was showing her some overdue affection.

"It was good, but I'm a little tired from working on your son's project. I whipped up some turkey burgers and home fries. The kids ate already, and ah, I'm pregnant again," she said as if it was nothing and continued to prepare dinner.

"For real, babe! When did you find out?" he asked. He loved making babies with Mahassin. This would make number three and counting.

"I took a pregnancy test earlier, but I still need to get it confirmed by the obstetrician."

"You made me so happy, Hassi and I promise to get you

a new home soon! I know it's hard living with Kim and I apologize. You forgive me?" he asked as he wrapped his arms around her waist.

"Of course, babe. In Sha Allah, this has been hard, but I trust you above all others except, Allah. You can always count on my loyalty," she replied.

"I know that's right!" he laughed and continued to show her affection as she prepared his meal.

The next day, Quadir had his weekly meeting. In the past, he only needed to meet once a month, but he stepped up to weekly meetings. He recruited many new jacks, and he had to make sure they knew he was God. Ever since the failed Gavin hit, he was overly cautious and somewhat paranoid. He didn't trust anyone in his camp and he was missing Hakeem more as the days passed. He realized too late he had a loyal rider in Hakeem, and he was sorry he didn't acknowledge it. He felt responsible for Hakeem's death and wished he did a better job protecting him when he was alive. Now, he was stuck with a bunch of bullshit. His suspicions didn't go unnoticed with his team. They were aware he didn't trust them because they were bussed and blindfolded to the meetings. None, would be able to out his location.

"How did we do this week? Quadir asked Bones when everyone entered the meeting.

"Better than last week, and we expect to double that next week! We have two new locations and we're getting major play from those college kids in Wynnefield. They buying up big weight and we have a new house in Hilltop. Those pussies over dere are soft ass shit and damn near bowed down when they realized we represented you! They want to get on now—you know play to stay!" Shy explained.

"That's what up! We can get into the money amounts later, Shy," Quadir replied because he didn't want him spitting out amounts. He was still a trainee and had a lot to learn as far as Quadir was concerned. "Now, regarding our good friend Gavin Douglas, do you have any good news?"

"My sister hasn't been able to contact his sister, but I did hear that his bike club is planning revenge on you. My girl said she was invited to the Welcome Home party they gave him last week, and they were plotting. She didn't hear all the details, but she said when she came out the bathroom, she heard them discussing it!" Abe eagerly responded.

"Yea, those bubblegum riders want some—burn the entire club down and kill all its members!" Quadir demanded. "And ah, don't forget their families. This city needs a friendly reminder of whose running shit and family members are target number one. Furthermore, you nigga's need to show and prove. It's been a month since I put the hit out and no one knows shit. Please don't show up at the next meeting empty handed," he warned. "Now, get the fuck out my face!"

Quadir was back, and he was ready to war. However, he was accurate with his trust issues. Rich was a new worker who regretted coming to work for Quadir. When he heard him put out the hit on the Savages, he had to do something. He had two cousins that were members of that club, and he loved his cousins. After the meeting, he informed his cousins and arranged to get his mom, baby mom, and kids out the city. They meant everything to him, and he wasn't about to lose them over his bad decisions.

CHAPTER 6

Gavin was happy and in love. Ciani kept her promise and married him. They had small intimate ceremony with the Iman. His mother, stepfather, sister, and brother were the only ones in attendance. The marriage took place in the comfort of their home, but Gavin had a surprise for Ciani. She assumed they would get married and that would be that, but Gavin planned a special evening for her. Christmas was a few weeks away, and Ciani did a good job hiding her excitement for his sake. However, he appreciated she humbled herself and put aside her beliefs. He had a surprise in the basement that his mom and sister put him down with.

"Babe, I love you!" Gavin said gushing on his bride.

"I love you more!" she replied meaning every word. Gavin thought she was the most beautiful he had ever seen her. Ms. Rhonda friend Khalifah made her dress and she produced a beautiful maternity wedding gown. It was exquisite, fitted at the top with a bubble bottom. Her headpiece was extravagant with lace and crystal appliques that made her look like the Queen of Sheba. "Babe, I got something to show you in the basement," Gavin said.

"I don't mean no harm, but since your brother been living down there, it smells slightly moldy," Ciani replied.

"I know—he stank right!" Gavin concurred, and they both laughed. "You're good, ma because we cleaned up." He led her to the basement, and she lost her mind when they got down there. Gavin had a beautifully decorated Christmas tree, but the wrapped gifts under it got her attention. The tree was filled to the brim.

"Babe, I can't believe you did this for me! You didn't have to go through all this trouble. Christmas is not for a few weeks," she said surprised and overwhelmed.

"You didn't have to marry me the way you did! I'm just sorry your father couldn't be here but as soon as the baby is born, we can make a trip to B-more."

"My father is coming for the New Year. I forgot to tell you. He said he'll stay until I have the baby in February. Anyway, enough about that—let me get to my gifts!" she said. Gavin surprised her with so many beautiful gifts for her and the baby.

"I was saving this for last," he said and handed her a jewelry box. Inside was a beautiful tennis bracelet and Ciani thought she'd go blind staring at it. The brilliance and clarity of diamonds stimulated her, and she wasn't a materialistic woman.

"Where am I supposed to wear this, Gavin?" she asked knowing she would never wear something so expensive.

"You deserve this and so much more, Cee! You proved yourself and I know I got a rider. I plan on spoiling you so get comfortable, wife."

"Okay, boss! I love you to the sun and back. Thanks for the Chanel bags too, I had a secret crush on those bags," she said happy and grateful for a man like Gavin. "How many carats is this thing?"

"I don't know, babe. I just purchased the most expensive bracelet in the store. Shine bright like those diamonds, Cee! You can have anything you want, love!"

"Thanks again for everything. I made a great decision marrying you! I'm about to blow up!" she joked

"You so silly, but that's why I love you.!Your heart is as pure as they come.

"You know I'm not perfect, Gavin."

"No one is, but to me, you come close. Listen, your man is hungry and not for food. You in the mood for some sweetness?"

"Anytime for you, babe!"

"What's going on down here?" Ms. Rhonda asked when she entered the basement.

"Your son is just too much! He surprised me with Christmas early. Did you have anything to do with this, mom?" Ciani asked. Ms. Rhonda had given her the okay to call her mom and that meant a lot to Ms. Rhonda. She knew Ciani lost her mother when she just a child. She proudly took on that mother figure role.

"You know, I may have had a little sump'em sump'em to do with it! You know how we do!" Ms. Rhonda replied being that cool mother that everyone could count on. She was beautiful, and she looked and acted like a young girl. She had long beautiful hair that hung halfway down her back, a caramel complexion and Ciani knew exactly why Kirk was head over heels for her.

"Thanks for everything. I don't know how I would've gotten through without you, Garin and Daddy Kirk!" Ciani replied.

"Did that fool tell you to call him that?" Ms. Rhonda asked.

"Yes, he specifically requested it," she replied.

"I need to have a talk with my aging husband! Anyway, I'll leave you guys alone. My show is about to come on and I cannot miss one second of it," she said and went upstairs.

"Thanks again, babe. I'm so happy!"

"Cool, now let's get out of this funky basement. I'll to talk to B-Smoove. I thought cleanliness was a number rule in the military. I guess he just said fuck it!"

"That's obvious!" Ciani agreed. When they entered the bedroom, Ciani slayed him with her pussy and rocked him to sleep. The next morning all hell had broken loose.

CHAPTER 7

Gavin was abruptly wakened to a thundering pounding on the door which startled him. "Who the fuck is it?" he barked. Ciani was woke and scared. She thought Quadir had found him.

"It's me! We got a problem and you need to get the fuck up!" B-Smoove yelled.

"This is some bullshit!" Gavin spats as he pulled up his pants.

"What's going on, babe?" Ciani asked scared to death.

"I'm not sure, but stay here until I find out!" he insisted. He met B-Smoove in the hallway. "What's so fucking important that you had to break my sleep, nigga?" Gavin asked agitated.

"Quadir just burnt down Aunt Rita's house! Thank God, she wasn't home, but the house is unsalvageable. She just called mommy. This nigga done went too far, Gee, and he's clearly sending a message!" B-Smoove explained.

"Where is Aunt Rita now?" Gavin asked concerned.

"She was at work, but I sent one of your guards to get her. She should be here soon. Bishop called, and we may have a lead on Quadir. They called an emergency meeting, and we need bounce now!

"Oh, my poor sister! Gavin, what is going on! You have fix her house or buy her another one," she demanded. "The morning news just showed her house in flames. She's lost everything!" Ms. Rhonda said when she saw her sons talking in the hallway.

"You know she don't have to worry about that, ma. I'll take care of everything!" Gavin replied trying to ease her mind. "Bee, give me a minute to get dressed."

"Where are you two going? I don't think you should leave," Ms. Rhonda protested.

"Ma, everything will be fine. I have to make a run, but we'll be back soon," he quickly replied and went into his room.

"What happened?" Ciani asked when he came back.

"It's not good, babe. I ain't gone lie, but it's nothing for you to worry about. I have to leave, but I'll be back soon. Quadir burnt down my aunt's house," he replied.

"Oh, my goodness, Gavin! Is she okay?"

"Yes, and she should be here soon. I need you to do what you do best and comfort her when she comes. She lost everything near and dear to her today."

"You know I got you and your family!" Ciani replied pleasing Gavin.

"I'm going to take a quick shower, babe. I think I smelled my mom cooking breakfast. You should go while it's hot," he suggested.

"Umm, I smell it. I'm on way," she replied, knowing she was about to tear up the salmon cakes and grits that Ms. Rhonda made.

When Gavin and B-Smoove arrived at the bike club, Gavin was surprised to see several members from other cities come through. He wanted to keep everything on the low, but he could use the help. Quadir went too far by burning down his aunt house. She lived alone and was a good Christian woman. She respected everything and everyone. He loved his aunt dearly even though she wasn't Muslim. She helped his mom raise them and they all looked at her as a second mother. She couldn't have kids of her own, so she took a special interest in her niece and nephews. He would buy her a new and bigger house, hoping that she would recover from the loss. He offered her a new house when he got out of college, but she was adamant she was fine with her three-bedroom row home in South Philly. Once inside, Gavin noticed an unfamiliar face in the crowd.

"What's good fam?" Gavin asked.

"Nothing really!" Bishop responded with frustration laced on his face. "Quadir is coming after all of us, so this is bigger than just you, Mag. I mean the world to my family and they depend on me as the man—you feel me. So, this bullshit ends now!" he spats. "This is, Rich, Troy and Tyrek's cousin, and he got something to say! Go ahead, Rich," he commanded.

"Quadir is planning to burn the club down tonight and kill all the Savages! He gon after families too. I'm here only on the strength of my cousins. I already warned my peeps, but I'm taking me and mines and getting ghost. I'm just giving you muhfucker's ah heads up!" Rich explained.

"When did this meeting take place?" Gavin asked, wondering how much time they had.

"Last night! He gave the orders and warned that if we didn't show progress, we were in jeopardy. Quadir is a demon—the devil himself! I was trying to make some extra money to take care of my kids and baby mom. I got a job, but it seems as if a nigga was just living paycheck to paycheck," Rich continued as he held his head down in shame, regretting his decision to work for Quadir.

"This nigga got to go!" B-Smoove barked. "Where is he laying his head at, Rich? That's the million dollar answer we're all looking for?" he asked losing patience with Rich.

"I'm a runner, just a corner boy! He don't let no one near him especially after Hakeem died."

"Where are the meetings held?" Gavin asked.

"Don't know that either. We're blindfolded before they take us to the meetings. Normally, it's like ten to a van and forty runners in the meetings," Rich replied.

The room erupted with chatter and the other chapter

members wondered what they had gotten themselves into. Gavin saw some of their expressions and that was exactly what he didn't want. However, he knew Allah would not be pleased with his next moves. He needed to transform his mind to deal with Quadir.

"This narcissist ingrate! He wanna war then we'll war!" Gavin said. He knew Quadir wouldn't stop until he destroyed everything he loved. He dreaded dealing with his aunt because he couldn't imagine how she felt.

"Listen, I don't where he is, but I know where his spots are throughout the city! I can give you those locations if that'll help, but I need to get a move on," Rich said. He was risking his life by snitching, but he had already put his life at risk when he said yes to the job.

"Nah, nigga you ain't gon nowhere! How we know you ain't setting us up. I don't trust this guy," B-Smoove protested.

"I don't give a fuck if you trust me or not! I'm getting the fuck out of this city and you stick around and see if I'm lying! I shoulda kept my mouth shut and just rolled out! I only snitched cause my cousins were in jeopardy and they already left! Bishop is the one who insisted I speak to you, Gee, but like I said, I could give zero fucks if you believe me! I'm getting the fuck outta this city!" Rich responded letting them know where he stood.

"Nah nigga, you ain't going nowhere! You need to go back, and act is if everything is normal," B-Smoove insisted.

"Fuck you, nigga! I already told you I ain't going back. And, for all I know these niggas could be watching us as I speak!" Rich spats

"Let me holla at him alone," Gavin requested, and everyone reluctantly left the room. "Listen, Rich, I feel you and I'm not trying to put your family in jeopardy. I appreciate you giving us the heads up and risking you and your family safety," Gavin said, trying to convey that he understood his fear.

"I respect you, Gee and all that you're trying to do for the hood. But, this nigga, Quadir is merciless!"

"Trust me, I know this, Rich! I barely escaped with my life, but I'm here and if you help us out, I promise to relocate you and your family. If you go back in and keep me informed, I'll give you two-hundred grand when this all over. That should be enough to start over," Gavin said in attempt to sway him on his side.

"Three-hundred and you got a deal," Rich responded because he wanted to have enough to buy a home and start a small business. He was tired of his kids and baby mom suffering from his hand. He wanted to marry Keisha, but he wanted to be sure he could care for her properly.

"Deal!" Gavin replied willing to pay the small fortune as a means to an end. "I need you to give me all his locations and runners. I don't want to go on a killing spree, but if I can get the head without the body count, I'm good with that!"

"Most of his runners are just as heartless as he is.

However, the new batch of workers are underage and naïve. I heard them talking and most are regretful. If you want to save some, they would be the kids to focus on. Quadir has them in training, pairing them off with journeymen," Rich explained. "If we gon do this, I'ma need some of the money now to get my family out! If something happens to me, I need to know my family is safe."

"I got you, Rich! What time do your shift start?" Gavin asked ready to get on with it.

"Eight, I'm on the night shift because I told you I had a day job until yesterday, when I quit. I do know where his new lieutenant, Shy live though," Rich replied.

"Okay, so this is how this shit is going down," he replied and quickly went over his plan with Rich. He spoke to his friends, gave them details and offered an out for anyone who wasn't feeling his plan. Unfortunately, he lost about ten men, but he wasn't mad because what he asked them to sacrifice was too much for the average man.

CHAPTER 8

Gavin gave Ciani a night to remember with his sex game and she was content and happy. He knew he needed to make her feel secure and loved because he was about to go to war and that would require him to be away from her often. He didn't let her in on the plan knowing she would protest and he would have to take time reassuring her. Instead, he told her he was fixing up the new location for Gavin Magnificent Headquarters. This time around, he planned to be discreet and low key. No one would know he owned the property, and he was no longer allowing people to come to the location. Only his employees would be allowed to enter the premises.

He received word that the bike club was burnt to the ground, but that was a part of his plan. He wanted Quadir to believe he was winning, so he would never see him coming. In addition, he needed to make sure Rich position was safe because he needed him. Rich called the next morning and confirmed his safety. He gave them all the information on Quadir's drug locations as well as his new lieutenant Shy address. Gavin and B-Smoove were on their way to meet up with his new killing team.

"You ready for this weekend?" B-Smoove asked once they were inside the car.

"I'm good, Bee, but I hate that people will die at my hand," Gavin fretted still uneasy about that part of the plan. Although, he had a plan that would decrease the number of casualties, he had to reinforce that to his team.

"It's us or them, brah! You need to get outta ya feelings, cause this shit is about to explode! I already told you to sit this one out, but I guess you got something prove!" he replied, ready to torture Quadir.

"Yea, I got that part. So, you think everyone is ready to bang? I mean, nigga's talk a lot of shit until it's staring them in the face! I know I can trust my Chapter, but I'm not so sure about the rest of these muhfucker's!"

"Muhfucker's is tired of this nigga, Gee! But, you can trust me and know that I got your back!" B-Smoove reassured.

"No doubt!"

When Gavin and B-Smoove arrived at Fairmount Park where his riders were waiting, he admired all the different style bikes. Riding was one of his passions that he stopped indulging, but he intended to get back into the game. Gavin was pleased seeing so many of his friends ready for war, but he was still uneasy about killing the city's youth. He needed to voice his concerns and make sure everyone understood the rules. Based on what Rich had said, Quadir new workers had regrets and Gavin had an offer for them. He needed to verify his team remembered his instructions. They parked inside the Plateau parking lot and joined the others.

"Magnificent, what's up, my man—long time no see!" Razor a member from the Baltimore Chapter greeted. "Man, what's good wit ya?" he asked.

"A lot of bullshit!" Gavin replied as he gave him a quick appropriate man hug.

Everyone greeted each other, and they discussed the weekend's event. Gavin made his demands clear and everyone was onboard. They had the location and instructions. After the meeting adjourned, they showed their asses on the bikes doing stunts and tricks. Gavin enjoyed the show and wished he had his bike. The display his friends put on confirmed that he would be purchasing a new bike, so he could join in on the fun. Gavin and B-Smoove left after the bike demonstration and went to get some lunch. It was freezing out and Gavin didn't miss riding in the cold.

"Gee, if you're not really feeling the plan, I'll handle it," B-Smoove offered after they were seated in the restaurant. "I know this isn't your thing—shit it ain't mines, but I will kill and steal to keep you and the fam safe!"

"Thanks, but this is my problem and I hate that you're even involved. No one can tell you shit with that hard head of yours, but I'm relieved you're by my side, because I don't trust everyone," Gavin replied.

"Bishop and Sharif will meet us there. Rich said it's

normally two per location, so four men to a location should be sufficient," B-Smoove confirmed, getting back to the plan.

"Yea, I just hope everyone makes it out alive, and no one tries to be the hero of the day. Salas said the vans should be at headquarters in fifteen minutes. After we eat, we need to make sure all the equipment came in," Gavin replied, reminding him.

Quadir was thrilled to hear the bike club was burned to the grounds, but he was angry, and disappointed in his workers and security. No one seemed to know where Gavin was, and his patience was running thin. His family life was a little more stable since he separated his wives and put them in their own apartments. However, Gavin was like a monkey on his back and he would not be satisfied until he met with his demise.

"Bones, what the fuck is going on with Gavin's situation?" Quadir spats when Bones the head of his security walked into the room.

"Honestly, I think this nigga skipped town and left the city! We found where one of his aunt's live and burned her house down. Unfortunately, she wasn't home at the time. His mom and sister's house are empty, and no one has come to either location besides the mailman," Bones explained. "Do you want us to burn down their homes?"

"Fuck no! He'll just buy them new ones. I'll need to make

some calls, because you nigga's aren't reliable!" he replied frustrated with his team.

"I understand why you're pissed, but it's like this nigga is a ghost. No one has seen or heard from him since that deadly day. That's why I think he left. You, yourself even said he was a punk so, I doubt he stuck around or planning revenge on you. Maybe it's time to move on," Bones suggested.

"Shut the fuck up, Bones!" Quadir barked. "I don't pay you to think or advise me. You haven't produced Gavin so there's nothing more to discuss regarding him. If I were you, I would be bowing down praising Allah for your life. The reason you get a pass, is because you saved my life. I'll take care of Gavin myself," he said and dismissed Bones.

After Bones left, Quadir woke up Kim to get some loving. Although, he knew she didn't love him, he got pleasure out of fucking her, knowing she hated it. A different man may have taken it to heart, but not Quadir. He enjoyed tormenting her. Once they finished the unwanted sex on Kim's behalf, he showered and left with his security team. She sat in a daze on her bed, but when she snapped herself out of her misery, she realized she could not spend another minute around him. She got herself together and made a call.

"Hello, Bam, can you meet me inside Jefferson Hospital Lobby? When you get there, I'll find you. Just take a seat a wait," she instructed.

"Why the hospital?" he asked confused.

"Why you think, but I'll explain everything when we meet in an hour," she replied.

"I'll be there!" he reassured. He always had a crush on Kim, but his money was never long enough for her lifestyle. She was a Boss Bitch before Quadir with her own business, car, and house. However, he would always be there for her.

*T*he weekend had arrived, and Gavin was anxious. He was ready to get this shit done, so he could get back to helping his community. He had faith in Allah that everything would go according to plan and that they would have minimal casualties. However, he knew his response to Quadir would cause a war, and he was ready. Quadir tied his hands when he came after him and his family.

"Bee, is everything ready for tonight? Gavin asked after breakfast.

"We good, brah! You need to stop stressing! The uniforms came in yesterday. Everyone have their orders and locations, Gee!" B-Smoove replied.

"What about the guns?"

"They were the first to come. All clean and untraceable," B-Smoove replied slightly bothered by Gavin persistent picking.

"I am relaxed, nig, just make sure shit is organized," Gavin jokingly replied.

"I gotchu, bro," he reassured.

"This shit needs to be quiet. I don't wanna ring no alarms," Gavin replied being cautious and meticulous.

"We all know that, Gee and we all on point! Ma, can I have some more waffles?" he yelled from the dining room table.

"You just ate three of dem muhfucker's wit ya greedy ass!" Gavin joked.

"I missed mommy's cooking. I'm being reintroduced to her delicious meals!" he replied joyfully.

"Here you go baby!" Ms. Rhonda said as she handed him a plate full of waffles. "I love cooking for my family and I'm so glad you're home, Gerald. I just wish I could get your sister out her room. I think she's becoming depressed being stuck in the house all the time," she warned, looking at Gavin.

"I'll talk to her, but y'all can go out. You just can't go to Philly and you can't go out alone. Trust me, ma, this will all be over soon. You'll be able to go home," Gavin responded.

"Actually, Gavin, ever since they burned my sister house down, I feel safer over here. I'm not so attached to the house that I can't move on. I'll think I'll look for a house here in Jersey. I like Jersey," she said. Gavin knew his mother was a trip, but he would give her anything she desired.

"Ma, I bought auntie that new home in South Carolina. Please don't make me feel worse than I already do!"

"Oh, that wasn't my intention! She'll never get over the loss but we're all happy you were able to relocate her so quickly."

"You got Ciani plate ready, ma she should be up by now?" he asked.

"She' s eating as we speak, baby! She got her plate first."

"Thanks for taking care of her for me. I appreciate all you do," he said, meaning it from the bottom of his heart. "Bee, I'll see you later. I need to spend some time with my wife."

Meanwhile, Kim had arrived at the hospital after she told Quadir she had a follow-up appointment. He only approved doctor visits and grocery shopping. Cliff, her security guard was cool, and she noticed he didn't report everything she did to Quadir. She had a feeling that he felt sorry for her. Normally, he would stay in the car and give her some privacy. She was hoping today wouldn't be any different. When they arrived at the hospital, he dropped her off and told her he would call to let her know where he was parked. Kim was thrilled because she would be able to speak to Bam without all the sneaking.

"Bam thinks so much for coming! You know I would not ask if this wasn't an emergency!" She explained her circumstance.

"You know I got you, ma. I'll text you when it's done. Do you need anything else?" he asked ready to oblige.

"No, that's a big one. Just make sure you talk to Gavin, but I'll call you when I relocate. Maybe, you can come spend some time with me," she added, knowing he was feeling her.

"Just tell me when and where, ma and I'm there," he

replied, and they parted ways. She still had some time to burn, but she decided to tell Cliff that they canceled her appointment. She needed to get home to make her escape. She already had her train ticket and her sister Lonnie was getting her money from the safe deposit box. She was eager to get her life back and rid herself of Quadir forever.

CHAPTER 9

Gavin and B-Smoove were on their way to his new headquarters. When he arrived, his team was positioned and ready. They were all dressed in utility and construction worker gear. Gavin obtained twenty utility vans that were loaded thanks to Silas. Although, he had completely left the game, he still had connections and Gavin was taking full advantage of it. Bill was feeling slighted because he had a desire to protect Gavin. When he heard Gavin had sought Silas help, he was somewhat upset. He called Gavin and expressed his concerns and Gavin had reassured him that he was good, but if he needed his help, he would let him know. However, Bill was working out some of Gavin's issues unknown to him. Bill had to settle a few issues with those Wall Street snitches. They ended up dead from an apparent overdose. Gavin didn't know he still had a few unresolved problems and Bill was making sure those problems disappeared.

"I see everyone is here and ready for whatever!" Gavin said as he greeted his team.

"We were just waiting on you, Gee. We been ready!" Bishop said.

"Yea, I'm hyped and ready! Let's get this shit rolling!" Pop concurred and everyone else agreed.

"Alright, cool! This is how this shit gon go down. I want everything to happen simultaneously. Does everyone have their intercoms?" Gavin asked.

"Yea, we good, Mag. Now, let's get this show on the road," Sharif said getting inpatient.

"Alight. Let's hit it!" Gavin said, and everyone conformed. However, B-Smoove and Gavin was heading to Shy's house. Gavin wanted to handle him personally in hopes of securing Quadir's location.

Fifteen minutes later, everyone checked in on the intercoms confirming their position. Gavin and B-Smoove had just arrived at Shy's supposed location. Luckily, they didn't have to wait long because minutes later, they saw him putting the trash on the sidewalk.

"This is us, brah!" B-Smoove said and hopped out the van. He didn't give Gavin a heads up and he proceeded to capture Shy. By the time Gavin got out the truck, B-Smoove had a gun to Shy's head enticing him to get into the van. "Hurry the fuck up, nigga!" he barked as he shoved him into the back of the van. Gavin pulled off quickly and headed back to headquarters. Everyone checked in around the same time, but Gavin found out there were five casualties. He figured that was still good considering, there could've been many

70

more. When they arrived at headquarters, Gavin opened the back of the van, and B-Smoove mean-mugged Shy, but Shy showed no fear.

"Nigga, you might as well kill me now, because I ain't telling you shit!" Shy yelled.

"Oh, your wish will come true, muhfucker! I think I'll let you marinate a while before I cook you ass!" Gavin replied. He knew Shy would never snitch, so he would have to die.

"Get ya punk ass out the van!" B-Smoove spat as he manhandled him into the building.

"Fuck you, nigga!" Shy yelled and B-Smoove punched him several times in the head.

When they entered the building, most of his team had arrived with the packages. Shy knew he was dead, but when he saw most of his runners in attendance, an anger crept inside like the Incredible Hulk. He decided he was going out like a true OG. *Fuck these snitch ass bitches*, he thought.

"Where the fuck is Quadir?" Gavin demanded.

"What the fuck I look like, *Gavin the Magnificent!*" he mocked, laughing at Gavin. "Like I told you corny muhfucker's before, I ain't telling you shit. Kill me now, bitches!" he said fearless.

"Nah, you gon die slow and alone since you're the man!" B-Smoove replied and punched him in the gut.

"Let me get some of that!" Bishop said as he knocked Shy out with a deadly blow. "This puppet ain't talking, so whatchu wanna do, my man?" he asked Gavin. Bishop knew

Gavin wasn't about the life, but he needed him to make a decision.

"Yea, bitch whatchu gon do! I see you got all my runners. You nigga's don't know the meaning of loyalty!" Shy said to his former team. "Oh, but you'll be reminded when Quadir come for you, and your families!" he spats.

"And, you're loyal to the worst form of man. Bee, take him in the back!" Gavin instructed then turned his attention to the young men his team had captured. But before he could address them, a few more of his team had arrived with another prize. Gavin appeared to be winning.

"Yo, Mag, we got all his shit! We found his stash house and cleaned him out! Whatchu want us to do with all this coke," Pop said when he entered.

"Hold it. I plan on giving it back to its rightful owner!" Gavin replied.

"Fuck you talkin bout?" Pop asked, scratching his head.

"You'll see, Pops. I don't want that shit, and I don't want none of y'all fuckin wit it either! You feel me! Everything will fall into place—trust me," Gavin said, trying to reassure him. Right then, they heard several shots coming from Gavin's office.

"Who the fuck is that!" Pops asked as he cocked his gun.

"Calm down, that's Bee, he's handling something in the back for me," Gavin replied.

"Please, we don't know where Quadir lives! We just

started working for him!" One of the young captured men said. At that moment, he feared Gavin more than Quadir.

"What's your name?" Gavin asked.

"Brian," the young boy replied.

"How old are you?

"I'm seventeen."

"Listen, Brian, I know y'all don't know shit about Quadir's whereabouts! Y'all are here for a different reason. I have something wonderful planned for your lives, so relax, we ain't tryna kill y'all! Excuse me for a moment," Gavin said, because he wanted to check on his brother. When he walked into his office, B-Smoove was wrapping the body up in plastic the construction workers left. "What the fuck, Bee! You couldn't wait, nigga! You see, we got a room full of witnesses and your inpatient ass just had to do you!" Gavin scolded when he saw his crazy brother cleaning up his own mess.

"He wasn't talking, and I know you would have a problem if I tortured him. You should be happy, big brah—quick and easy!

"Yo, I think we got a lead on Quadir!" Bishop yelled, bursting into the room. "I'm just waiting on a call, but if this lead is any good, all our problems will be over soon!"

"That's what's up! Now, we just need to get ready for phase two," Gavin replied, ready to get his life back.

Quadir had just wrapped up his conversation with his wives and felt content that they were safe. He always kept his own place for his own sanity and the other women he entertained. His mood was bright that night because he had finally got the beautiful Natalie's attention. She agreed to have dinner with him even after he told her she had to wear a blindfold. He had one of his security guards pick up her up, and he was just waiting for her to arrive. She was different from Kim and Mahassin and he enjoyed conquering those boogie corporate bitches. Natalie fit that description and he was ready to knock that chip off her shoulder. Meanwhile, he had no idea his business had been ripped from under his feet. However, a few minutes later, Bones shattered his world with the news.

"We need to get you the fuck outta here, now! Someone stole all the weight from the stash house and the workers are missing. No one can find them, and five lieutenants are dead too!" Bones explained in a panic.

"What the fuck you mean all my weight is gone?" Quadir asked trying to wrap his head around what Bones what dishing. "Where's Shy?"

"He ain't answering his phone, but we need to move you to a safer location. This place may have been compromised.

"Call, Andre and tell him to take Natalie back! Call my wives security and tell them to be ready! Let me get something real quick," he said and left the room. He opened the safe in the wall and grabbed his money and other valuables when he entered his bedroom. He grabbed all his personal identification, and they quickly left. He didn't have his four-men team, because he sent Andre to scoop up Natalie.

When they got outside, his security surrounded him and quickly made their way to his SUV. A raggedy homeless man approached them begging for change, but before Quadir could get into the car, the man had simultaneously killed Quadir security team, catching them off-guard. Quadir was left bare and alone.

"This ain't no request, nigga. Get ya punk ass inside the car!" the unknown bum spats, hitting him upside the head with his gun. He shoved him into the car and drove off fast, leaving skid marks in the wind. Once he drove a safe distance, he pulled into a vacant lot, tied Quadir hands and ankles, and placed duct tape over his mouth. He drove off and called Bishop

"Yo, I got that package, but it ain't cheap! It'll cost you a hundred grand!" he said when Bishop answered his phone.

"You'z a greedy nigga, Bam, but let me holla at my manz!" Bishop replied and hung up the phone.

Bam would do just about anything for Kim, but when she confided in him and explained what she was going through, he was eager to assist. She wanted him to get to Gavin's people and give them Quadir's location, but Bam had his own plans. *Why get someone to do what I'm capable of doing himself,* he thought. Her a little problem could've been taken care of had she told him earlier. Kim's plan was to disguise herself, so she could leave without being seen, but he had a better idea, he killed her security guard, so she could walk out the front door. They made plans to meet at a hotel in Jersey and she promised to hit him off. That was the break he needed. He penis was well endowed and strong. He was ready to introduce her to Heaven. However, he wanted more than sex, he wanted the whole package and with this money he was about to get, he hoped it would seal the deal. Though his money was short, he lived a comfortable life for a single man with no kids, but he desired more. He used to kill people for a living and get paid a nice dollar, but the young black youth started killing each other on a regular, and he lost most of business. He took his money and opened a Barbershop and that's how he met Kim. She rented the top of his shop for her salon and she didn't fuck with just anyone. He hoped everything went quick because he was anxious to see her.

"We got him, Mag!" Bishop said when he ended the call. "But, this nigga trippin, talkin bout he wants ah huned grand for this piece of shit!" he explained.

"He already cost me two hundred, but you know what, call him back and tell him he got a deal. I'm ready to end this shit tonight! I need to make a stop to get that money real quick! Tell him to bring him to this location," Gavin said and handed him a paper with the address. "Make sure his drugs come along for the ride."

"Right away!" Bishop replied.

Before Gavin became a legitimate business man, he hid his money in several locations. He never retrieved the money, and it sat for years. He knew he had at least five-hundred grand lying around. He still needed to pay Rich, but Rich told him the hit was successful, he would stay in town. So, he was waiting to see the outcome.

Before he left, he addressed the young men. "Listen up! Y'all need to get comfortable, because you'll be staying for a while," he explained, and they all had confused expressions.

"This is some bullshit; my girl is expecting me home! She's been freaking out about me not spending time with her. I know she gon leave me if I don't show up tonight!" One of the hostages said shaking his head.

"You telling me you ain't got no game with your lady! You hear him, Bee!" Gavin joked. "Trust me, by the time I'm through with you, she'll be laughing instead of bitching. You're not here by accident. I planned for your stay, so you can help yourself to those blowup beds and sheets over in the corner. Food will arrive shortly. I need all the minors to write down your parents or guardian's name on a sheet of paper. I'll go into more detail when I get back," he explained.

"Let's get the fuck outta here!" B-Smoove demanded.

"Sharif, I need you stay here and run this shit with the other Chapters. Make sure they have plenty of food," Gavin instructed.

"Damn, why I gotta babysit and miss all the fun?" Sharif

complained. "But I got you, Gee," he replied ready to assist in any way.

"That's what's up!" Gavin replied and left with B-Smoove, Bishop, Pops and twenty other local members. Gavin didn't want the other Chapters involved in the next phase. Quadir was their problem, and this was personal.

He called in a few favors from Salas, who was reluctant at first, but he eventually came around. He remembered the conversation he had as they drove to his stash house. Salas was truly out the game and paid a hefty price, but he still had important connections who would accommodate him. Silas was thrilled with his new American status. Gavin thought about their recent conversation earlier in the week, and Silas was one hilarious Mexican.

"Gavin, my fren, how ju been?" Silas asked.

"Thankfully, I'm healthy, but I need your help," Gavin replied.

"It depends on what you need, amigo! Ju know I don't roll in the same circles no more. I may not be able to help—if ju know what I mean!"

"I know, but I think you can," Gavin countered.

"Are you calling me on a secure line?"

"Of course!"

"What ju need?" Salas asked, hoping he could be of assistance.

"I need like twenty utility vans with uniforms, and a

secure location to handle that monkey on my back!" Gavin explained.

"When ju need these things, Gavin?"

"Yesterday, nah, but on the real, I need them immediately!"

"Okay, I'll get back to you today. And, Gavin, I hope this will bring an end to your little problem," Salas replied, knowing Gavin was going after Quadir. "Listen, when the dust settles, you should come to Cali. I have a beautiful mansion in Beverly Hills and I would love for you and your beautiful woman to see it. Bring the whole family! I love this country and I love Annabella! I know she would love to see you."

"You're right, but not about Annabella! I'm sure she's done with me, but Ciani deserves a vacation. After she has the baby, I'll make that happen," Gavin assured.

"Sounds good, amigo! I call you back," he replied and ended the call. When Salas paid for his freedom, he paid for Gavin's and Quadir's too, and they were all free from the Cartel.

Gavin, B-Smoove, Bishop, and Pop arrived at a house in Glenolden Pa, one of his stash locations. He instructed the rest of the crew to go straight to the loading dock. The ride would take about an hour, and he wanted to get there quick. In addition, he was a bit nervous with them carrying all those bricks of cocaine on the Jersey Turnpike. He warned the driver to follow the speed limit.

"I'll be right back," Gavin said, exiting the car. He walked up the steps to the single-family farm style house and rung the bell.

"Oh, thank you, Sweet Jesus! Gavin I've been so worried after I saw the news! I tried to call you, but your phone kept going straight to voicemail. Get in here, boy and let Ms. Mattie feed you!" she said ready to cook an entire meal for him. She was sorry she didn't bake that cake yesterday.

"It's good to see you, Ms. Mattie, I can't stay, but I promise to come back and spend some time with you. You can make me that famous banana pudding I love so much!" Gavin replied when he entered the house. Ms. Mattie had to be approaching seventy and her home décor represented her age. Her house was clean and immaculate and smelled like brown sugar. "I need to pick up something I left," Gavin explained.

"Help yourself, baby, I haven't been in that room in years! I keep it locked and I don't let anyone go inside. I mean, it's not like I get visitors, but the room is the same way you left it. I can't remember where I put the key though. You may want to check the top drawer of that buffet table," she said.

"Thanks, but I still have my key. I'll only be a few minutes."

"Take your time, Gavin. I'm just pleased to see you alive

and well!" she replied, and he ran up the steps, because he was running behind.

When he unlocked the door, he entered the room he stayed in after he graduated college. The room was exactly how he left it. He moved the twin size bed and pulled up a few of the wood floorboards. He reached under the floor, pulled out the silver security box, and opened it. The money was intact and all there. He quickly placed the floorboards back and moved the bed back into place. He went back downstairs, and Ms. Mattie was standing there with a bag of wrapped food.

"I know you don't have time for me to make you a proper dinner, but here's some fried chicken and potato salad I made earlier. Don't be a stranger, Gavin!" she said and handed him the bag.

"I promise, I won't, Ms. Mattie. I want you to take this money and go on a vacation. Looks like you don't get out enough," he replied and handed her ten thousand dollars.

"Oh no, baby, Ms. Mattie can't take that! You've done enough for, old Ms. Mattie when you paid off my home after my grandson died! You know he was all I had, and I appreciate you stepping up and paying for the funeral. I didn't know where I was gon get the money, but I had faith in God! Ms. Mattie don't need this!" she protested, refusing the money.

"Ms. Mattie, I want you to do something that you only dreamt about, and I won't take no for an answer!" he replied, placing the money on the table. "I have to go, but I promise I'll visit again soon. I'm about to be a father, Ms. Mattie and I want you to be a part of that." He kissed her on the cheek and left quickly with the silver box in hand. "Let's roll!" he said when he entered the car.

When Gavin graduated college, he was a millionaire, but ninety percent of that money was illegal. So, he had to hide his money and Ms. Mattie's house was one of the few locations he used, outside of his safe deposit boxes. He was close friends with her grandson Malik, and when he was killed in a car accident, he felt bad for, Ms. Mattie. His mother died giving birth to him and Ms. Mattie raised him from a baby. She didn't have other children, and she was a good Christian woman. He used to sleepover when he was younger, and he loved it. He thought Malik lived in a mansion, and Ms. Mattie would always cook and let Malik and Gavin do whatever they wanted in the house. They would sneak in girls and Ms. Mattie never snooped around, or tried to bust them. When he heard Malik died in a car crash, his heart went out to her and he took care of her financially.

"I can't wait to meet the infamous, Quadir!" B-Smoove said breaking the silence in the car. Everyone was in deep thought and anxious, but he was fired up and ready.

"I can't wait to see this nigga face when he sees who rocked his kingdom!" Bishop added. "This hit is for the betterment of the city and everyone involved. This is justified!" he continued.

"Yea, this man thought he couldn't be touched, but we'll see who has the last laugh!" Pop said.

"Fuck what he got to say, I want to hear this nigga plead for his life!" B-Smoove spats and Gavin glared at him wondering if the military had damaged his brother. He appeared to eager to take a human life. Although, Gavin understood what fueled him, he hoped this was temporary.

"Hold up, y'all, Bam is calling me," Bishop said. "What's good, we straight?" he asked. "You there already—what the fuck you flew! Yea, we had to get that food together for you. We should be there in fifteen minutes," Bishop said and ended the car. "He at the spot waiting with Quadir!"

"So is everyone else. The drugs made it safely, so we need to push it! Tray just text me," Pops said.

"The GPS says it's less than five miles, so we should be there in five minutes," B-Smoove said and sped up.

Quadir was regained his senses, but the blow to his head still had him shaky. He moaned unintendedly from the pain, but when he realized he was tied and bound, he knew it was the beginning of the end. He would never let them see him sweat and he was preparing himself mentally for death.

"You woke, nigga! I'm sorry to say it won't be for long, but you enjoy your last few minutes on earth! Let me open the windows, so you can smell the lovely ocean breeze!" Bam taunted when he heard him moan. Quadir couldn't respond due to the duct tape stuck to his lips. "Oh, and don't worry about, Kim! I'll make sure she's well taken care of in your permanent absence. I'll start tonight when I'm tearing up her pussy and breaking in that ass. You fucked with the wrong the girl, when you took her hostage, but no worries, we'll get that rectified immediately!" he said, continuing to anger Quadir. "See, I would've killed you myself, I didn't need to go through all these dramatics. The thought of fucking, Kim was motivation enough! But, the more I thought about that shit, the more I realized how valuable you are! So, here we are!" Bam said as he checked his rearview. "And, here they are! Time to clock out, nigga!" he said and jumped out the SUV.

Quadir was furious knowing Kim had set him up to die. He knew she didn't love him, but he never believed she would betray him to that magnitude. As his captor led him into the vacant loading dock, he was overwhelmed with fear. Bam took off the duct tape, and when he entered the dock, he spotted Gavin and his fake goons.

"Y'all pussies ready to play—it's a good day to die!" Quadir greeted.

CHAPTER 10

When Bam brought Quadir inside the loading dock, he tried to show a brave face, but it was obvious he was shitting bricks. Gavin took a moment to enjoy his stress, but he had no intentions on prolonging his death. He didn't want Quadir tortured or taught a lesson, no, he just wanted him dead and he wanted to be the one to complete that mission.

"I see you got jokes, nigga! But I'm happy to know you're ready to sleep permanently!" Gavin retorted. "We'll try to get to you there as soon as possible. Pop, bring in his shit!" Gavin demanded.

Quadir was hoping they didn't have Mahassin and his kids because that would break him. However, when he saw Pop and a few other men push in his drugs, he breathed a sigh of relief. He watched as they brought in all his dope. There must have been at least a hundred bricks of cocaine, and he was confused to why they robbed his drugs only to bring them to him.

"You niggas are geniuses! You rob my empire then bring it to me. Fuckin rocket scientists!" Quadir said mockingly.

"You ain't never lied about that. We thought you'd like to

go out like the real G you think you are. See, we can't have these drugs flooding the city, so we thought you like to have your possessions on hand," Gavin replied, but B-Smoove trigger finger was itching.

"Gavin, you always been a soft nigga, ah bitch nigga, so let's get on wit it!" Quadir spat.

"Your wish will be granted. Pop, tape as many bricks as you can to this dead man!" Gavin demanded, and Pops grabbed several bricks and taped them to Quadir's body. By the time he was done, Quadir's full body was wrapped in his drugs and he could barely stand.

"You must be the dumbest muhfucker's I ever seen in my life! You got my product, and you're about to let it wash away with the waves. Gavin, you ain't learned shit—soft ass nigga!" Quadir spats. Gavin had had enough of Quadir's mouth. He grabbed the gun out of B-Smoove hand and shot Quadir in the stomach and he fell to ground. He laughed hysterically, and Gavin shot him four more times, but he made sure he didn't kill him. "Bishop grab those gloves and y'all prop this nigga up! Tie his ass to the bricks! It's time to be done with this piece of shit! I have a vacation waiting!" Gavin said. Pops and a few other men tied Quadir to his bricks of cocaine. He yelled out in pain from the manhandling and gunshot wounds.

That burning pain began to affect Quadir, and he knew he was in the thick of it. It was ironic that he found himself in the same position he had placed so many. However, he wasn't scared no more, and he was ready for death.

"You nigga's can suck my dick!" he yelled as a last defense.

"I heard you don't have one!" Gavin replied and shot him in the head. He had a flashback of the kidnapping and torturing, and all that anger and hurt resurfaced. His was going to let him drown in his own blood, but he was over that shit. He needed to make sure Quadir wasn't breathing when he left the dock.

"Damn, brah, you good?" B-Smoove asked, shocked at Gavin's actions. He was slightly upset because he wanted to be the one to end Quadir's life. Nevertheless, he was proud of his big brother but concerned. He killed many people defending America, but he knew his brother wasn't a killer until that day.

"I'm good! Let's get on with it so we can bounce!" Gavin said.

Gavin's team used rope and tape to secure Quadir's dead body. They pushed him and his drugs into the Atlantic Ocean and watched as the waves drifted him further out to see. Once he was out of sight, Gavin paid Bam and they all headed home. However, Bam had a hot date, and he was anxious to prove himself to Kim. His day was productive, and he was leaving with a small fortune. His plan worked out much better than Kim's

*L*ater that night, Gavin had withdrawal symptoms from his first kill. He was fine until he got home. The entire house was asleep, and he was relieved, because he threw up several times that night. He couldn't sleep, and he prayed longer than usual when 4:00 am arrived. After prayer, he felt slightly better, but he had regrets. Killing a man wasn't something Gavin ever thought he would entertain. Murder had tainted his many accomplishments, but Quadir tied his hands. He wasn't sorry Quadir was dead, but killing one of Allah's children left a stale taste in his mouth. He finally dozed off around six that morning. Ciani let him sleep until noon before she startled him out of his sleep to tell him to turn on the news.

"Oh, my God, Gavin. Wake up, you need to see this! They found Quadir dead in the ocean!" she yelled, and she turned on the TV. "Somebody beat me to the punch and sent him to Hell early!" she continued hyped as she tuned into the news.

This just in! Quadir Miller, a known drug dealer was found murdered in the Atlantic Ocean near Wildwood New Jersey. Police say he was tied and bound to over one hundred kilograms of cocaine! We spoke to several residents who did not want to be shown on camera, who verified Quadir Miller was a ruthless drug dealer who ran the City of Philadelphia for years. Sources close to us reveal the FBI had been investigating him, but unable to make anything stick. Police have no witnesses or suspects, but we will keep you updated on this breaking story.

"I hate to say it, but that's great news—right?" he asked, trying to be as cool as possible and feel her vibe.

"What? That's fantastic news! I know, I'll have to repent for feeling so redeemed, but I'm not in that state of mind right now. Aren't you happy?" she asked as if he bumped his head.

"I don't really have no feelings about it, bae," he replied on his chill.

"Gavin, this man almost broke you! When I saw you laying in that hospital bed, I could barely look at you. I was horrified, so I prayed and asked God to avenge you. My prayers are answered—thank you, Heavenly Father!" she said with praying hands.

"This is a blessing for our family, babe. Hopefully, everything will go back to normal. I bought my mom and Kirk a new house not too far from here. Garin will stay with them for a while," he explained.

"What about your brother? Is he's sticking around?" Ciani asked, hoping the answer was no.

"Not for too long, bae I'll find him a place soon. Listen, forget about that right now. I want to take my wife to dinner and the movies tonight. Whatever you want to see," he said, summoning her back to bed. "Come lay with me, Cee. I need to bond with you and the baby," he said relieved everything went down as planned. He had big plans for his future. He snuggled and loved on Ciani for the rest of the afternoon. She declined the date because she was exhausted from carrying the baby. Gavin understood, he just hoped her sweet spirit returned after the baby. Since Ciani shot him down, he went back to his headquarters to deal with the young boys.

Over at City Hall, Congressman Chapman had just saw the news, and the wheels began to spin inside his head. He called Representative Linwood as soon as the news ended. "Linwood, did you see the news?" he asked when he answered the phone.

"Yes, I wonder who killed the infamous Quadir," he replied. "This shit is crazy, because whoever did this was sending a message. This is a victory for our city!" he said satisfied.

"I know who did it, I just need to prove it. I don't want to talk over the phone. Can you meet for lunch tomorrow?" he asked.

"If who you suspect is Mr. Douglas—the answer is no. I think enough harm has been done to our law enforcement. Agent Gray is still awaiting trial, and we don't know what he will say," he said reminding him that they could still be implemented.

"He won't talk. He'll lose his job and pension, but he'll walk free—trust me!" he replied confidently. The judge had reassured him, but he wasn't sharing that with Congressman Linwood.

"I guess you know something I don't, which isn't unusual. Listen, I want to discuss funding for this after school program I'm working on. I'll be happy to meet regarding that," he said, letting him know he was not interested in his little goose chase.

"Fine, Linwood. I'll have my secretary call you when I'm available!" He ended the call without allowing him to respond. He called his assistant into the office and told him to get Private Detective Morris's number.

Unbeknownst to him, Congresswoman Tamika had become superb at spying and listening in on calls made from the office. She was planning on resigning in the next couple of weeks because she was fed up with nothing being achieved. She realized she could make a better change by directly being involved in the community. However, she needed to warn Gavin that Dave was still obsessed with him. She took a chance and called the number she left the message on, and surprisingly he answered.

CHAPTER II

After Gavin arrived at headquarters, his phone rang. "Good evening, Mr. Douglas. This is Congresswoman, Tamika Butler," she greeted when he answered.

"Good evening, Congresswoman! It's been a minute, how are you?" he replied.

"I'm good, but it's imperative I speak to you as soon as possible. I need to discuss the future of this city. I was hoping we could meet tonight," she explained. She needed to discuss the issue in person.

"Tonight, is kinda short notice, but if it's important to you, I can make time."

"Great, can you meet me at the Pub in South Philly by nine o'clock?"

"Sure, the one on Packer Ave?" he confirmed.

"Yes, that's the one."

"I'll be there," he responded curious as to what she really wanted. He could read between the lines and knew it was more to it than that.

"Great! I'll see you there."

When Gavin got off the phone with the Congresswoman, he went inside to address the young men. When he entered the building, he was surprised to see everyone was on their chill. However, when they saw him they gave him his full attention.

"What's up, everyone. I hope you all had a good night sleep. I'm here today to assist you with your future goals. Some of you may not be interested and that's cool too, but I think once you hear what I have to say, you'll see you have nothing to lose," he explained.

"I need to call my mom," One of the underage boys blurted.

"I know. Sharif, did you get their parents number?" Gavin asked.

"Yea, here's the list of numbers and addresses. I was going to start calling, but I didn't want to overstep—ya feel me," he replied.

"That's cool, and thanks for staying here all night. If you need to handle some business, B-Smoove can take over for a while," Gavin offered.

"Yea, I got some things to do, but everyone one else is cool. We were taking shifts, so no one gets overwhelmed."

"That's what up, fam! I'm grateful!" Gavin replied.

"No doubt!" he replied as he gathered his things and left.

"Listen up, I need to call some of your parents and let them know what's up. Basically, this is what it is—you all inspired me to move in the direction of this new mentor program. I don't have all this shit figured out, but what I do know, if you stick with me, you'll all have substantial jobs in a couple of weeks. I need y'all to be patient and open minded. I plan on being personally involved in the success of this project. I just need a couple days to get everything in order," he explained.

"If you're talking about offering us jobs that we can support ourselves—I'm in," one of the older boys said.

"That's good to hear, young man. This week, I'll spend time getting to know you, so I know who and what I'm dealing with. This Friday, we're all going on a field trip. I want to introduce you to a different way of living. The life I'm about to show you only happens in your dreams, but it's obtainable," he explained "So, do I at least have your interest?" he asked, and everyone said or shook their heads yes.

Gavin spent at least an hour building up rapport and reassuring them. When he finished, he went into his office and called the female members for assistance. Everyone he was able to contact said they were in one hundred percent. Once he received confirmation, he began calling all the parents on the list Sharif gave him. Two of the moms went ballistic, because they had been worried to death about their sons. However, once he told them who he was and what he's trying to do, they came around. One mother said her son couldn't come back until he showed a change, a couple of mothers didn't care one way or the other. He was exhausted when he hung up the phone with the last parent because she wanted to talk his ears off. He was sad to know that none of them had reliable fathers.

He spoke to the members of his Bike Club who was helping Sharif babysit. They came up with a plan to take shifts and everyone was down for the cause especially when he told them he would pay them. Gavin was sorry Ciani was out of commission because this was right up her alley and she was valuable. Nevertheless, he decided to keep her out of the business until the baby arrived.

"Bee, tomorrow, I'll need you to go to pick up some TV's and whatever video shit is out now. I'll have Bishop order twenty beds. I just figured out exactly how to use this space. Instead of calling it *Gavin the Magnificent*, we'll call it the *Magnificent Leadership Mentor Program*. Get my old employees numbers and see if they feel comfortable coming back. I had a great team before all this bullshit," he instructed.

"I got you, Gee. But, check this out. After I handle your business tomorrow, I need to handle mines. I haven't had no pussy since I've been home, so I'll need a few days to myself," he replied.

"As long as you don't bring em back to the house, but I understand. I think Ciani would go ballistic because she doesn't do well with other women," Gavin warned. He smiled thinking about his lady. When she was pissed, Jesus was nowhere to be found. It still amazed him how she would snap in an instance. She kept him guessing at times, but he enjoyed her spontaneous ways.

"Fuck I look like. I'm looking for a place now, but I'm meeting up with, Brenda with her fat ass. She sent me a naked pic and I'm ready to tear that ass up. She got a nice house in Mt Airy."

"Brenda, I haven't seen her in years. I remember she had ya ass whipped, ready to rob banks and shit!" Gavin joked.

"Man, fuck you! No bitch ain't never had ya boy sprung!" B-Smoove countered.

"Listen, I have to meet someone real quick. You sure you don't mind staying until Sharif gets back?"

"Yea, I'm sure. Oh, I almost forgot, Bishop called and said Rich want to holla at you about a job. I guess he decided to stay put."

"Alright, I thought after he got the money, he would be long gone. I'm out."

Gavin said his goodbyes and headed to South Philly. He wondered what was on her mind, knowing it had to be important. He drove well over the speed limit down 76 East, anxious to see what she had to say. He pulled into the parking lot and walked into the Pub. He glanced around the room and spotted Tamika sitting at the bar. He walked up and slightly startled her when he touched her shoulder.

"Gavin, I'm so happy you could make it. I'm sorry I was in a deep thought and you scared me. Have a seat. Can I order you a drink?" Congresswoman Tamika asked.

"No thanks, love. I don't really drink, but can I buy you a drink?" he replied as he sat on the barstool beside her.

"Let's move to the booth in the corner right there," she said wanting more privacy for what she had to discuss.

"Sure, I'll follow you," he said as he allowed her to lead. He knew he was wrong for looking at her ass, but those pencil skirts she wore, were dick teasers. When they arrived at the table, he allowed her to sit first before he joined her.

"Gavin, I won't beat around the bush. Congressman Chapman is coming for you. He called Representative Linwood after they discovered Quadir's body. He believes you're involved. He wanted to feel him out, but Linwood wanted no parts of you. After, he hung up on him, he called a private detective," she explained, whispering the entire conversation.

"Man, fuck this shit!" Gavin said frustrated. "I can't seem to catch a break!"

"I know it appears that way, but I was so happy to hear you were alive and doing well. I have the private detective's information, so maybe you can track him before he tracks you—if you know what I mean. After today, I won't be able to help you anymore in that aspect, because I'm resigning in two weeks. I'm trying to help this young mother, and I want to make sure she gets the money that's owed to her from the city. The decision won't come until next week," she explained.

"I love that, Congresswoman. I can see the passion for Philly in your eyes."

"Please, call me Tamika. And, yes, I love this city *and* the people, and that's why I'm leaving politics. I'll be more productive on my own. I've made a few connections, and I found that I can raise more money and resources outside of politics," she replied.

"This must be fate, Tamika. I have a new headquarters and mentor program for young men. I don't have many workers and my wife would normally take the lead, but she's indisposed with pregnancy," Gavin laughed.

"I didn't know you got married, but, how would I? Congrats on the marriage and baby! That's a wonderful blessing, Gavin. Family is everything. I love my husband and daughter, but sometimes I feel guilty for living a good life when, so many people are struggling. The change begins with folks like us," she said optimistically.

"That's right, shorty. Like I was trying to say before, I could use your help. When you quit you Uncle Tom job, come work for me. I'm sure I can be competitive with your salary. In addition, you'll be helping your community." Gavin offered.

"I was hoping you had a lead for me, but I never expected a Job offer," she replied ecstatic.

"So, is that a yes?"

"Yes, it would be my pleasure. What does the job entail?"

"Whatever you see fit. I need you for everything. The

plans are still in the making and I could use your help and advice. We can put these great minds together and build something magnificent!"

"Awesome! In the meantime, I'll keep an eye out and an ear open. Here's the information about the private detective. I better get home before my husband think I was on a hot date with a handsome man," she joked as she gathered her things and stood up.

"He wouldn't be wrong about the handsome part," he countered with a smile.

"Indeed!" she replied. Gavin escorted her to her car and headed back to pick up his brother.

The news of Congressman Chapman had him uneasy, but he decided to deal with the problem immediately. He would never allow shit to linger and build to the point of Quadir. It was time for the good congressman to learn a lesson. Gavin had lives to change in Sha Allah. When they reached home, his mom warmed up dinner, and they ate. He checked in on Ciani and she was asleep as usual. So, he went into his office and called Bill.

"Hey, son, what's good," Bill said when he saw Gavin's number on his phone.

"Life!" Gavin replied smiling because Bill was funny as shit trying to be down.

"You should meet me in LA, Friday. I have a few people I want you to meet," Bill suggested. "I think we can make some money," he encouraged.

"Wow, that's crazy! I was about to tell you I'm coming to LA Friday. But, check this out, I have another problem. Someone hired a private detective to investigate me. I can go into details when we meet, but I'm asking for help." Gavin humbled himself because it was extremely hard for him to ask for help.

"Your problems are my problems and we can't have that. You know I always do what I can for you. I can't wait to see you. I'll send the jet."

"I need a jet that'll fit twenty-five people. I have another favor to ask. I have this new mentor program and I want them to experience the good life. I believe if they see it and live it, they can achieve it. You think you can set something up when I come because I'm bringing them with me."

"Anything for you. I think I can handle that. This is exciting! I'll get my peeps on it right away," Bill replied.

"Thanks for everything. I'll see you, Friday," Gavin replied and hung up.

For the next few days, Gavin worked long hours setting up his headquarters. He made great progress in a short time, and he was feeling much better about everything. His nightmares were becoming less, but that might've been because he wasn't getting much sleep. His headquarters had been turned upside down with construction. Although most of the construction was already complete, he needed walls built for his four classrooms and five dorm rooms. His former employee Wanda came back, but the others were still scared. She was a great help in ordering supplies and keeping the young men in line. They all appeared to respect and like her, and she took some weight off his shoulders.

"Listen up, we're going on a field trip tomorrow. We'll be flying to LA," Gavin said passively as if he told them they were going to the museum.

"LA, that ain't no field trip, Mr. Douglas. That's a real trip!" Diggy said, calling him by the name Gavin insisted on. He was one of the under-aged kids and he was excited.

"You're right, Diggy. I'm about to introduce you to a world that you only dreamt about. Here's the thing, don't let what you see distract you. Money is only good as the user. I have money and I could live anywhere in the world. I don't have to do what I do, but I never let the money control me or my way of life. Shit, I lived with my mom before I met my wife! The point is, the money doesn't consume me, but is sustains me. I need money, so I can help you succeed," Gavin responded.

For the next few days, Gavin spent time organizing the trip, getting permission slips, and making sure they had clothes and personal items. He was building up a rapport with the young men which encouraged him. He hoped the trip would seal the deal, and he could begin building their minds.

CHAPTER 12

Gavin, B-Smoove, Bishop, Pop and the mentored arrived in LAX Friday afternoon, and Bill had a tour bus waiting. The young men were all excited when they boarded the high-end bus with all the expensive trimmings. Gavin felt good providing an experience he knew would change their lives. An hour later, they arrived at a spectacular mansion in Bel Air. The house had spectacular canyon and city views.

"Alright, we arrived, and I need y'all to be on your best behavior. We have the house for the weekend, so have fun, but don't break or steal anything. I'm not trying to say y'all are thieves, but you just never know. Don't embarrass me," Gavin warned before they exited the bus.

When they entered the house, they were stunned silly and everyone was ready to play. They took a few minutes to choose their rooms before meeting Gavin at the pool. Bill always made an impression. He made every effort to impress and a full staff was waiting to cater to their needs.

"Mr. Douglas, all that food is for us," Curtis asked. It was his eighteenth birthday, so the trip was right on time.

"Sure is, Curtis! Happy Birthday and enjoy yourself. And, ah I better not see no minors drinking alcohol! For the five that's legal, enjoy!" he cautioned.

"Damn, we can't drink, and we don't have no smokes! This trip is going to be boring!" Hassan spats. He was nineteen years old and withdrawing from being sober all week.

"Drinking and smoking weed is weak, Hassan, but I understand you little niggas are feigning," Gavin replied.

"Yea, we are. Ain't weed legal over here in Cali though?" Nyfese asked. "I don't mean no disrespect, Mr. Gee, but we want some weed. Trust me, that will relax everyone," he said, trying to make Gavin understand the addiction was real.

"I'm not cosigning to that shit, nor am I providing drugs to make you feel better. I thought bringing you out here would be motivation enough, but I guess I was wrong!" Gavin sighed, agitated at the young men. They all seemed to agree with Nyfese, but he had little sympathy.

"Mag, let me holla at ya real quick?" Bishop asked. "Listen, Mag, I know you tryna help these young men, but the reality is most kids and these young adults are smoking the chronic. I see the statistics everywhere and that's why more states are adopting the idea and making it legal," Bishop reasoned.

"Do you smoke, Bishop?" Gavin asked, wondering why he was trying to convince him.

"Actually, I do smoke occasionally! But, don't get twisted,

I don't smoke that chemical weed and I don't have a problem with weed," Bishop explained.

"You're by yourself on that one, but I feel where you're coming from. I'm not about to support the weed smoking, but I won't interfere if I happen to smell that shit. However, no weed for the minors and make sure they don't drink. I don't give a fuck if they fall out from withdraw!" Gavin said, trying to ease up, but he was responsible for the minors. He had to get parental permission to bring them on the trip.

"I hear you," Bishop said as he joined the others.

Everyone enjoyed the rest of the afternoon, eating, drinking, swimming, and acting like fools. However, when Bill and a few of his associates arrived, they brought a boatload of women with them. The young men perked up, and the women had their full attention. They were high-class escorts, all beautiful and sexy. They catered to the young men while Gavin handled his business with Bill.

"Like I was telling you earlier this week, Congressman Bitch Ass Chapman hired a private investigator! My friend, Congresswoman Tamika informed me. You know I don't like to ask for help, but I'm tired, Bill. I just want to do me without all the problems," Gavin explained.

"Don't worry about a thing, son! I expected something like this would happen after I saw the news. I won't ask if you had anything to do with that because I already know. That was a big hit, and the FBI was on it. I saved you ass, Gavin!" he quarrels. "I don't mean to be a prick about it, but

I need you stay the fuck out of trouble! Now, as far as Dave Chapman is concerned, I'll handle him too! I've been ready since your unfortunate situation. He'll learn a life shattering lesson just like those Wall Street rats," Bill continued. He was breaking down all the things he done for Gavin, but not for gratitude. He loved Gavin and needed him to understand that's why he did it.

"I appreciate everything you've done, Bill—from the heart!" Gavin said, placing his hand on his chest.

"I know. Listen I've been holding on to this damning information about your local politicians. Even the beautiful congresswoman!"

"Tamika Butler! What could you possibly have on her?" he asked intrigued.

"Oh, nothing as bad as the rest, but she's a weed head! We got a tape of her copping weed. And, I must say, she's very creative in disguising her identity. She dresses as lesbian and after she gets the package, she changes clothes a mile or so before she reaches home. Once the household is sleep, she retreats to the backyard and get blaaaaazed!" he emphasized.

"Nah, I can't believe that!" Gavin replied floored from the discovery. "Yo, she works for me now. You think I'm good?" he asked still shocked.

"Unless you have a problem with weed, that's the worse we found. I think you two share the same passion but,

Chapman, that scumbag will be taken care of immediately!" Bill reassured.

"Thanks, man! You always look out like no other. I'm forever indebted to you and you're the closest thing to a father I had in years," Gavin replied, showing his gratitude.

"Those words mean the world to me, son. As long as I'm capable, there won't be much out of your reach! Now, tell me about this program you're founding," Bill said flattered. When Gavin expressed himself that was the green light she need. "Oh, before I forget, Annabella called and said something about Silas being upset when he heard you were in LA. You should contact Annabella before you leave, son."

"No doubt," he replied. They spoke about Gavin's program and their businesses, before he joined the others. When he entered the massive game room, he spotted Bishop and Pops playing pool. "Where is everyone?" he asked slightly drunk.

"Fucking somewhere," Bishop laughed.

"They must be in heaven by now! The women swooped them up, and it's been quiet for a minute. I was waiting for you come back. That beauty sitting at the bar is waiting for me! She said she's gon suck the black off my dick!" Pops said.

"Suck the black off? That shit sound like it'll hurt. Yea, good luck with that!" Gavin said jokingly. "Seriously though, where are kids? They better not be fucking or smoking weed!" Gavin warned. He knew it was likely they weren't virgins, but he didn't need child molestation added to his plate.

"They at the pool, but I think they snuck some smoke. The weed just magically appeared," Pop's replied, and Gavin knew Bill was responsible. "The buffet is history! Those little nigga's ate up everything! Shit, you spent damn near a grand feeding them for the week! We need to come up with a food package plan or your ass gon go broke!" he laughed.

"I'm winging this shit, but when we get back, I'll figure it all out and we'll put this program on the map. For now, I need to keep my word, and figure out how to strengthen their minds," Gavin responded. "If my wife was available, this wouldn't be an issue," he replied, missing Ciani. She was righthand on the last project. He missed working with her and he hoped she would consider coming back though he never asked. He didn't want her stressed or overwhelmed with working.

"Oh, before I forget," Pops remembered. "I know you're married, Gee, but there's a nice little sumptim waiting in your room!" he said with a bright smile.

"Nah, I'm good, Pops. Bishop you take her," Gavin offered.

"Hell nah! My wife can smell week old pussy—after many showers. I love my life even though I played roulette often. I'm good, but I'm surprised at you. I guess that beautiful wife changed the dog in you," Bishop smirked.

"Nah, Allah changed me, but she enlightened me and directed me to my true passion. She's a keeper and worthy of my loyalty," Gavin explained. He meant every word, but their sex life was nonexistent. She was uncomfortable with her body, so he told himself after the baby things would go back to normal. However, the more he thought about it, the more he was tempted. "You know what, ain't nothing wrong with getting your dick sucked!" he rationed, trying to convince himself it wasn't the same as cheating.

"Nah, nigga, it's a good thing. Maybe you forgot, but ah, that pretty little package waiting, may be able to refresh your memory," Pops agreed, being a bad influence.

"Don't do it, Magnificent!" Bishop warned, calling him by his biker name.

"You're right, Bishop! Fuck was I thinking about?" Gavin replied. "I'ma tell her to bounce." He left with that intention in mind. However, when he entered his room, he was greeted with a gorgeous fat ass. And, when she turned around and gave him a full view, the situation turned deadly. Her breasts were full, and the hardness of her nipples were asking to be sucked. Gavin was hypnotized by the way they bounced with just slight movements. She was stunning, and her face was clear and smooth like a baby's ass. She was the total package and Bill knew what pleased him. He always had a special treat for Gavin after he copped his candy, and he didn't disappoint that night.

"I've been waiting for you!" she seductively said. "I hope you don't mind, but I had to start without you," she said and began masturbating. "Aaaaaaah, I can't wait for you to stick your Congo cock inside my garden of cherries," she moaned.

Calm the fuck down Jeffries, Gavin thought, talking to his penis. *This is just another pussy,* he continued thinking to himself, trying to control the growing stiffness.

"Listen, sweetheart, this ain't gon work! You should leave!" he strongly stated like the lion he was.

"Leave, you don't want me to leave!" she responded and got off the bed. She walked towards him slow as she massaged her nipples and rubbed her clitoris. *Fuck fuck...fuuuuuck!* he thought. "Don't be nervous or shy, daddy. I promise not to do too much damage," she whispered and began massaging his crotch area. "Oh my, what do we have here!" she said bending down and unbuttoning his jeans. *Jeffries, you a bitch! No, don't do it,* he thought, but it was too late. The big butt escort had wrapped her entire mouth around his penis. She was of Hispanic decent, but she didn't have an accent. She sucked and swallowed him whole making him weak and then she went in for the kill. "I want to feel you inside me, but before that, I need you to lay down," she instructed.

"Nah, just keep sucking!" he protested.

"Okay," she said as she resumed sucking and massaging his balls. His legs were getting weak as she delighted him, and he wanted to sit down to get the full experience since he was already fucked.

"Yea, let's go to the bed," he said as he held onto his pants and made his way to the bed. He sat down, and she was all over him. She put his penis between her voluptuous breasts, squeezed tight and sucked the tip as she glided her breast up and down his massiveness. "Aaah, yea that feels good!" he whimpered. His sighs of passion encouraged her to magnify her skills, and he was a goner.

"I want you to fuck me with that big dick!" she demanded. She pushed off him, sat on the floor, and spread her legs like eagle wings. She pushed two of her fingers inside her vagina and twirled them around. Gavin was at the brink of insanity. "Come on, daddy. I need ah little help!" she said licking her other finger as she pricked her nipples. *This is some bullshit. Jeffries, you let me down with ya weak ass*, he thought. "Grab that magnum size condom on the bed stand and strap up, because I'm going to fuck you like you're a king!" she boasted.

"Okay!" Gavin said, caving to her will. He was seconds away from having blue balls and her vagina was calling Jeffries. He quickly grabbed the condom, ripped it open and slid it on. He swooped her up as if she was a baby and placed her on the bed. "This is what you want?" he asked, holding his dick in his hand.

"Yeeees!" she yelled. He pulled her body to the edge of the bed and slammed inside her walls. "Oh yes, yes, daddy, it feels so good!" she cried. Gavin took all his frustrations from the past few months and annihilated her vagina with voltage-like shocks. *Damn, this guy can fuck*, she thought as he filled her with pleasure.

"Your turn—to fuck me like a king!" he said panting from the extensive workout. He laid on the bed and summoned her. She stood over him, squatted down on his penis, and twerked slowly. However, when she found her groove, she steadied her position and gave him the ride of his life. Normally, Gavin could maintain some control in that sensitive position, but she was bouncing all over his dick as if she was a gymnast. When she did a hundred and eighty degrees turn on his penis, he was impressed and in bliss. As she rode his frontier from the back, he was able to regain control. He sat up and pulled her body into his. "Come here," he demanded as he pounded rapidly inside her walls.

"Oh, daddy you're the best I ever had! Don't stop—doooon't stop!" she begged as he took her body to an unknown galaxy. However, she positioned herself for the twerk ride and twerked his ass into orgasm Heaven.

"Aaaaah," he said as he released inside the condom.

"Damn, love you got skills!" Gavin said satisfied from the wonderful orgasm.

"You're not too bad yourself! Actually, I must admit, you were wonderful!" she replied, boosting his ego.

"You want to go for round two?" he asked, knowing he had already compromised his marriage.

"I would love that, but, Bill only paid for one fuck! I'm not paid by the hour, and I have another engagement. But, thanks for the offer," she replied.

She dressed quickly and left Gavin sitting on the bed holding his deflated penis. He felt as if he'd been pimped. He was disappointed in himself and prayed this never reached

Ciani. He had to admit that it was one of the best fucks of his life. *She was spectacular*, he thought. He never caught her name, but she left a lasting impression on him. However, once the thrill died, the guilt surfaced. He was still dealing with killing Quadir and now adultery tainted his character. He was anxious and unable to sleep, so he poured himself another drink, hoping it would rock him to sleep. He wanted to forget the whole week, and he was ready to go home. The next morning, Bishop knocked on the door, waking him.

"Come in," he yelled.

"Mag, everyone is waiting for you. I mean, I don't blame you for sleeping in late, after the night you had. We all heard that shit!" Bishop joked.

"What time is it?" he asked.

"Almost noon, and Bill said he'll be here shortly. He said he's bringing some of his business friends too. You need to get a move on, my man," Bishop explained.

"Alright, I'll be out soon," he replied, and Bishop left. He took a shower and joined the others. When he entered the dining room, everyone had eaten, but the housekeeper brought him a hot plate of food. It took him a minute to notice that all eyes were focused on him. Once he did, he said, "Fuck is wrong wit y'all?"

"Ain't nuttin, Gee. It's just we know someone had a good night," Pops responded, and the room erupted with laughter.

"I don't know what you're talking about," he replied as he took a bite of the turkey sausage on his plate. Bill and his business buddies walked inside, and Gavin was relieved for the distraction. He was already feeling sorry for himself. "Bill, what's up?"

"What up, son? We bout to be bout it-bout it," he responded sounding corny.

"Bill, please stop already!" Gavin laughed. "I was just finishing my meal."

"When you're done, you all can meet us in the living room," Bill replied and left with his friends.

"Why does he call you, Son all the time?" Bishop asked.

"He thinks he's my father, but he is the best father figure I've had since my dad passed away. Kirk is cool, but he's in it for my mom," Gavin explained.

"You think he wants a new nephew? I could use a rich uncle—you feel me," Pop said.

"I'll second that!" Sharif concurred. He spent of the most time babysitting.

"You muhfucker's are crazy. Let's go see what's on his mind," Gavin said and they all followed him into the living room.

"Gavin, come, I want to introduce you and your friends to my friends," Bill said when they entered the room.

"Come on y'all, don't be shy," Gavin instructed.

Once the ice was broken, Bill and his five friends took a sincere interest in Gavin's new mentor program. They encouraged the young men and treated them as if they were equals. These men were billionaire's and Gavin appreciated the time they spent with his young crew. They were receptive and gave the billionaires their full attention. By the end of the meet and greet, Gavin had secured jobs for his eighteen and older group. He wasn't worried about the rest because he could take care of that personally. Gavin and his connections astounded the young men, and they all pledged their loyalty to him. After the meeting, Bill asked to speak to Gavin alone.

"Listen, Gavin that issue with Congressman Chapman will be resolved tomorrow. Also, I took care of the private detective too. His interests have changed, and he's now on my payroll. He'll be useful in the future," Bill explained when they entered the home office.

"Good looking, Pop's! You always got my back," Gavin replied gratefully.

"I will always have your back, Gavin. But, ah what did you just call me?" he asked wanting to be clear he heard what he thought.

"Pop's, you mean, yeah I said it!" Gavin laughed.

"I don't mean to sound like a little bitch, but that one word was the best thing I heard in a long time!" Bill gleamed.

"You're the closest I'll ever come to having a father, Bill. And, I hope we can continue to build on this relationship. I'm more than grateful for everything you do to support me. I know I don't tell you much, but if it weren't for you, who knows how my life would've turned out—thanks again, Pops!"

"Pops, I think I like the sound of that. Anyway, I'm working on this new business endeavor, but once I get all the details, you know I'll put you on. Another thing, I don't want you to get mad when you hear about my party. I'm not inviting you to this party, because I don't want you influenced by all the evil that will take place," he explained.

"Evil, and what party?" Gavin asked.

"I'm having a Billionaire Party. Last week my net worth went to a billion dollars, and the Billionaire Club is hosting this party for me."

"Why I can't come?"

"Because, I don't want you involved with these types of men! What you're doing for your city and community is honorable, and jealous worthy. I need you to stay on track. What these men have to offer comes with sacrificing your morals and values. Trust me, this isn't the party for you."

"I trust you, Bill and if you say it's a no—then it's a no. I'm glad you warned me though, because had I found out about it through someone else, my feelings might've been hurt."

"I'm glad you understand. I have VIP tickets for Six Flags and a bus tour of the Hills. Normally, they wouldn't be allowed to tour in the area, but I made some special arrangements. I think it'll be fun. The bus is outside ready whenever you are. Take the young lads and have a great time at the park," he instructed as he handed Gavin the passes.

"Thanks again for everything, and I'll call you once I reach home," Gavin said, and they parted ways.

Bill and the other moguls left, and Gavin's small trip was a success. He took them on a small shopping before heading to the park where they let loose. later that night, they headed over to Silas mansion. Gavin reached out when he was at the park, and Silas invited them all over for drinks. When they pulled up to Silas mansion, they were impressed and so was Gavin.

"Gavin! It's good to see you, my friend. I see you got a whole basketball team with you, come in, I've been waiting for you all evening."

"Follow us, y'all," Gavin commanded, and everyone entered the Victorian style mega mansion.

When they entered, there was a party in session and everyone was enjoying themselves as Spanish music played in the background.

"You see, Gavin! This is the life you could have. Why don't you bring the miss's and the baby out here? This is a much healthier environment for all!" he said trying to convince him.

"Thanks, but they have too many earthquakes out here, but I'll definitely bring the fam out. This house is beautiful though."

"Gracias! Oh, here she is! Annabella, I was just about

to send the troops after you!" he said when Annabella approached them.

"I'm sure you were, Papi. Gavin, it's good to see you and from what I hear, you're not staying out of trouble. I'm just relieved, I not responsible anymore," she greeted.

"Will you ever let that shit slide, Annabella! I mean, shit happens in life and none that was under my control. As I recall, I never asked for your help, but I'm sorry if you're still harboring feelings, love!"

"You two, stop it! Let's not argue on this special occasion," Silas replied, attempting to put an end to the quarrelling. "Take your friends to the backyard, Gavin and meet me in my office. Most of the party is there," he instructed.

When they reached the backyard, the party was in full force, and everyone was ready to get their Salsa on. "I'll be right back. Remember, behave and enjoy yourself," Gavin cautioned. "Silas, what's good?" Gavin asked when he entered his office. Annabella was with him, and Gavin instantly became tense.

"Everything is good, my man. Annabella and I are married now, and she makes me very happy!" he replied and kissed Annabella on the lips. "Annabella, you have something you want to say to Gavin?"

"I'm sorry for being an ass. You're right, I need to let our past go. Please accept my humble apology," she said.

"I accept, and I hope this will be the end of it. I respect you for all you tried to do for me—know that," Gavin responded.

"Good, now that we have that settled, are you okay? When I heard about Quadir's murder and how they found him, I knew it was you, Papi!

"Damn, how the fuck everyone knows that?" Gavin asked agitated.

"The drugs, fren! No one else would've released those drugs the way you did. I see you're uncomfortable with the conversation so, let's move on," he suggested. "Annabella get us some drinks and, food. I want to spend some time alone with Gavin."

"Sure, Hun, I'll be right back," she said and hurried off.

"You two! But, forget about that for now, tell me what's going with you," he said.

They talked for almost an hour before wrapping up the conversation. Silas was pleased to hear he was alive and well, and Gavin was ready to get home to his wife. When he joined the others, they were in full swing, dancing, laughing and having a great time. Gavin didn't want to end their fun, so he let them party until Silas kicked everyone out.

"Gavin, I hope to see you soon. It was a good meeting everyone—safe travels," he said when he escorted them out.

"I'll call you when I get back," Gavin replied.

While on the plane ride home, Gavin noticed Samir was quiet and looked distracted.

"Samir, why you look so sad?" Gavin asked, wondering what his problem was.

"Yo, Mr. Douglas. I told you before that I was in jeopardy of losing my girl. She just text and told me she packed my shit, and not to come home. I appreciate the job and everything you're doing for me, but I need to fix this shit. I can't lose my lady," he explained.

"I'm sorry to hear that, Samir. I feel you on that, youngin because I love my lady to the moon. When we get back home, we'll figure out something," Gavin reassured. Samir had showed Gavin a picture of his lady and she was on point. He understood why Samir wanted to keep that relationship intact.

"Thanks, Mr. Douglas. I appreciate anything you can do."

"I got you, and we can stop with the, Mr. Douglas. I know I told y'all I to call me that, but I think we've built up enough rapport for you to call me Gavin. That goes for the minors too. And, I want to thank y'all for being on your best behavior and making what I'm trying to do, look good."

"We got you!" Samir replied, and everyone agreed.

CHAPTER 13

When they reached home, Gavin was hyped and eager to get the ball rolling. He explained that the mentor program was still mandatory even for the ones who had jobs. He wanted to touch base with Tamika to see if she was ready to start. He called his lawyers and requested a meeting. He needed to get the paperwork completed. When he entered the home, Ciani was in the kitchen cooking, which was a welcome sight. She hadn't cooked since she got pregnant, and Gavin thought that was a good sign. However, when he greeted her with a hug, she was somewhat distant.

"What's good, wifey?" Gavin asked as he kissed her neck.

"Nothing, just tired of carrying this baby," she replied rolling her eyes. "And, I'm tired of you not being around. I tried to be patient and allow you to get your footing, but I think you forgot about us," she continued as she rubbed her belly. "And, when are we going to apply for the marriage license? It seems you forgot all about that shit!" *Oh, she's mad*, Gavin thought.

"I'm sorry, bae for not being here for you, but we will get

the marriage license in due time. What's the rush anyway!" Gavin replied getting agitated.

"What's the rush? Are you kidding me with your selfish self? I agreed to this marriage only if you got the marriage license, but it's becoming clear you have no intentions. Excuse me!" she said barging past him and leaving the food on the burners.

"Yo, the food is still cooking, Cee! Stop acting like a child and come back!" he yelled, but that request went on deaf ears.

He turned off the pots and pondered what just happened. After a few minutes, he figured it was the pregnancy taking its toll. He decided to leave it alone and handle his business. He went into the office and started making calls. He called Ms. Jones, Muhammad, and Deacon Barry, and they all agreed to help. Ms. Jones agreed to work for him, but Muhammad and Deacon Barry could only lend assistance due to their own projects they were working on. He called Tamika Butler to see if she was available yet.

"Ms. Butler, how are you, love?" he asked when she answered the phone.

"I'm great now that I'm free! Did you see the news?" she asked.

"Nah, I just got back from out of town. What happened?"

"Two videos surfaced of Congressman Chapman with underage girls, and since then, three more have come forward with an accusation of sexual assault!" she explained.

"Get the fuck—I mean for real!" he said impressed with his unofficial adopted dad. Bill was the truth.

"Yes, so you don't have to worry about him coming for you. He has his own mess to clean up. Everyone is asking for his resignation, but he hasn't commented yet."

"I ain't mad at that, Ms. Butler. So, when can you start, love!" he asked, needing her expertise immediately.

"My last day here is Friday, but the husband is taking me away on a needed vacation. I can start in two weeks," she replied.

"Damn, I was hoping you could start sooner. I need your help with getting the paperwork and permission to run this mentor program. I have twenty right now and I'm just winging this shit," he explained.

"Okay, I'll tell you what, I can do a couple of hours after work. However, I can only give you two hours, but when I get back, I'm all yours," she replied, wanting to help him out. She believed in him and had confidence they could make a serious change in the youth.

"Hey, I would take fifteen minutes if that's all you had, so two hours is great!"

"Good, send me the address and I'll be there this evening around six."

When he got off the phone, he felt relieved, and he believed he was on the right track. He had people who he trusted willing to put in the work. Between his bike friends, Ms. Jones, Wanda and Tamika, he had a great team. He thought about how nothing was beyond Bill's reach. Congressman Chapman could kiss his ass. Gavin prayed there were no more haters coming for his throat. He decided it was time to smooth things over with Ciani. She was right to be mad at him, but he had been pumped since he came out the coma.

"Babe, I'm sorry I haven't been there for you the way I should. I don't mean to take you for granted," he said as he sat on the bed beside her. She was laying down staring at the walls in a daze. "Earth to Ciani," he said waving his hand in front her face. "Tell the aliens that got you in a trance that I will fuck them up!" He got off the bed, walked to the wall she was staring at, and began to fight the aliens. Ciani couldn't help but laugh. He did dumb shit like that all the time, and she loved his corny sense of humor. "Aaah, there she is," he said when she laughed at his poor acting skills.

"You are stupid, but I love you. Why you play so much?"

"Because, I love you and I want you to be happy. I promise to spend more time with you and Gavin Jr," he comforted before sliding inside the bed. Her mood brightened, but he could still feel the tension. Gavin realized he was placing his marriage in jeopardy, which was one of the stupidest things he's done. "Baby, trust me, I hear you. We will get the marriage license soon, and once the baby comes, we'll be one small happy family. You, me, and our blessing from Allah," he said, trying to reassure her.

"I love you so much, Gavin, but I hope you mean it. I hope your passion to help everyone else, doesn't exclude us," she replied as she placed his hand on her belly. "You've been so preoccupied since you came back to us."

"Never, that will never happen, baby! And, when you're feeling like I'm not supporting you, just let me know. You mean the world to me and I value you in every way."

"Same here! Okay, I'll get back to my Christmas dinner," she said satisfied with Gavin.

"Christmas is tomorrow, Cee, but I thought we already celebrated," he said, over Christmas, but trying to be sensitive to her feelings.

"We did, but you know I'm not the best cook, so I was doing a few practice runs. Last year, your mom made the turkey, but I'm not making one this year," she explained.

"Okay, babe. I'm going to catch few z's because I need to meet Congresswoman Tamika later at the office."

"Oh, what you need to meet her for?"

"I hired her since you're indisposed now. I think she'll be an asset. I'm sure she knows who's who in the city and that will only help my program!"

No fucker, I know who's who, she thought slightly jealous, because he was moving on without her. "That's nice," she responded dully.

"And, guess who else is joining us—Ms. Jones. She told me to tell you hello," he added, knowing she wasn't thrilled about the congresswoman. He figured he would tell her about Ms. Jones to keep her mood stable.

"I love, Ms. Jones. You definitely can't go wrong with her on the payroll," she responded and went back into the kitchen. Her mood deflated, but she tried to shrug it off and get back into the Christmas spirit. However, she had to start over with the mac and cheese she began, because the noodles were too soft. Gavin appeared to be moving on without her and he didn't even know it.

Gavin was uneasy when he arrived at the office to meet Tamika because he knew there was still some tension between Ciani and himself. Nevertheless, he still had a job to do, and he needed to get the mentor program stabilized. When he walked inside, everyone was busy playing games, on the phone, or just sitting around talking shit.

"What y'all doing?" Gavin asked already knowing the answer.

"Nothing, Mr. Douglas—I mean, Gavin. We just chilling. We learned a few interviewing skills and how to adapt in the workforce," Darius said. He was one of the chosen who received a job from the meet and greet.

"Yea, who taught y'all that?" Gavin asked.

"Ms. Latisha," he replied.

"Tootsey Roll came and looked out," Sharif said when he didn't recognize the name.

"For real!" he said surprised and trilled.

"Yea, I called her and asked her to come through, because

I'm tired babysitting these mugs," Sharif said. Initially, he was just interested in getting rid of Quadir, but he was onboard with Gavin a hundred percent.

"I'm starting to feel the love," Gavin said. "I'm expecting Congresswoman Tamika. Send her in my office when she gets here."

"She's already here. Bishop took her to your office before he left. Listen, Gee, I'm willing to do the work, but you need more people to take care of these shifts. Preferably the night shift. I can't be missing out on pussy—you feel me," Sharif said, hoping he had a plan to get some more workers.

"That's why the congresswoman is here. Trust me, Sharif, this shit will be organized soon enough. You know everything happened quickly. Give me a couple of weeks, but I will get more people to cover the night shift," Gavin assured and headed to his office. "Congresswoman, I'm so glad you could make it!" he said when he entered his office.

"Please, just call me Tamika. My congresswoman days are ending, and you're my new boss," she said, trying to make a good impression.

"You got a point there. Okay, Tamika I need your help, advice, expertise—whatever you can offer," he said, hoping she could rescue him before his ship sank.

"Tell me about the program and all that's involved.

"Basically, I'm trying to save as many young men as I can. I want to offer them the opportunity to partake in job training, interviewing skills, tutoring, and anything that prepares them for life. Also, I want them to stay on the premises, so they don't get distracted by the streets. There's so many ideas I have, I just need you to do the leg work. I need you to be my right hand and take the lead with the paperwork, permits, or whatever," he explained.

"Okay, I'll make some calls and get the information. But, I can tell you this will be expensive, but hopefully we can get some contributors," she replied.

"I'm not worried about the money. I still have money in the bank from supporters that gave to my last headquarters. I'll give you my lawyers and accountant's numbers, and you can contact them about what's left. We can start there, but I'm willing to do whatever to make this work."

"I admire your passion, Gavin, and I'm looking forward to helping you build this into something great! Tomorrow, I'll have more information since I know the direction you're going in. But, ah when I start full-time, where will I sit? I see you still have construction going on," she asked. Gavin noticed she was sitting in the same spot where he found Shy's body slumped over. He had to have the floors in his office re-cemented and they were still bare. "Gavin, you okay?" she asked.

"Yea, I'm good. The construction should be completed by the end of the week. Let me show you your office. Once it's complete, you can choose whatever furniture you want. The walls will be painted tomorrow, and the floors should be installed too!"

"Great, lead the way!" she said, and he showed her the office next to his. He had three in total.

After the tour, he escorted her out and chilled with his team before heading home. Ciani was in her feelings and he needed to change that. When he entered the room, she was watching tv. He sat on the bed, pulled her face to his and kissed her passionately. Ciani got aroused, and she allowed him to slip in from the back. They made love and Gavin was confident they were back.

CHAPTER 14

*T*wo months later, Ciani gave birth to Gavin Jr. and his mentor program was up and running properly. He was a proud father and husband. Ciani pushed Gavin Junior out as if it were nothing. She was only in labor for an hour before their bundle of joy entered the world. Gavin was in awe of her performance and he had a new level of love for her. However, her feelings differed. Although he tried, his mentor program took precedence even if he tried to deny it. Along with his businesses, he added three dogs to the mix. He picked up two pits from the pound, and he recently added a Belgian Malinois Shepard who he named Cranberry Vampire. *What the hell*, Ciani thought when he introduced her to the dog. She tried to put on a happy face, but she was pissed. *Another dog to distract you*, she thought. He spent most of his spare time training the dogs, and she was over it. She held her tongue because she knew it relaxed him, but she didn't know how much longer she could play along.

On the business end, Tamika took the lead on the legalities and made Gavin's job much easier. Initially, he wanted the kids to live at the camp for two months. Unfortunately, he only received permission for them to stay during the summer vacation, holidays and after school. Also, the entire program was reduced to six weeks. Tamika believed they could reach their goals within that timeframe. However, his first group had stayed for two months and they all had decent jobs. He hired his minors and placed them at his restaurants throughout the city. Life was good, and Gavin was content.

The program was structured and offered a range of resources to assist the young men. Gavin worked hard to keep the program low key because he had learned his lesson. Most of his inquiries about his program came from referrals from the young men or his staff. He realized the hard way he could not single-handedly save the entire city. He was finally comfortable staying in his lane and making a difference where he could. They were readying themselves for the new additions. Since he couldn't take in the kids, the new group were all eighteen and older. However, he had an after-school program that offered tutoring, support services, and after-school activities. His staff was terrific and even the first group came back and mentored the teens. Gavin had their respect and loyalty, and he enjoyed going to work.

"Gavin, did you see the news this morning?" Tamika asked when he came inside.

"Nah, I missed it. What happened?"

"Congressman Chapman hung himself! I guess he couldn't live knowing his career and life was over as he knew it. I am sorry to hear he took the coward way out though," she explained.

"I'm not! Actually, I have no feelings whatsoever." "I don't blame you, Gavin. On another note, I wanted to discuss something with you if you have the time," she requested.

"I always have time for you!" he smiled. It took some time for Tamika to figure him out. Initially, she didn't know if he was flirting, but over time she realized he was a silly gentleman with no sexual intent involved.

"Thanks! I know we have our hands full with the men mentor program, but I was hoping you would consider adding young women and girls to the mix. They suffer too and have a direct impact from the men's actions. I was just thinking we shouldn't exclude them," she explained.

"You know, I never thought about it that way. I think you are on to something, love. I don't really have time with the new baby, but I trust you. Once you iron out all the wrinkles, get back to me with the details."

"Oh, thanks so much! I definitely will and congrats again!" she said and left satisfied. Gavin valued her opinion, and she still was getting used to him saying yes. When she was a congresswoman her ideas got denied often. She loved her new position, and she was making more money.

Gavin stuck around to meet the new group and provide encouragement. After the meeting, he went to lunch with B-Smoove to discuss his future. He wanted to know what he planned on doing with his life. He was an asset to *Mentor Magnificence*, the name of his organization, but he knew B-Smoove wasn't as passionate about it as he was.

"Bee, what are your plans for the future?" he asked after they ordered.

"I'm not sure, Gav. Honestly, I'm just trying to enjoy my freedom for a minute. But, I was thinking about opening a barber shop. I learned how to cut hair in the military. I don't want just any shop, Gee. I want a full-service shop where the brothers can get some pampering too! Shit, I love getting pedicures and treated like a king," he replied.

"That's what up! I'm surprised but proud. When you get serious, you know I got you, brah!"

"Yea, I know that!" he replied as he took a big bite of the turkey burger on his plate. "But, ah, I do need your help with finding a place to live. I know Ciani is tired of me living in the house and I need a place of my own to entertain the ladies—you feel me!" he said and took another bite of the burger.

"No doubt!" Gavin replied indulging in the Salmon with lemon garlic sauce.

"Thanks, but ah did you see the news today?" he asked.

"Nah, but I already heard about Congressman Chapman," Gavin replied.

"Who the hell is, Congressman Chapman? Oh, he must one of those reps that came for you. Nah, this isn't about him. Three teenage boys got hit last night down north. Two dead and one in critical condition. They're saying it was drug related, and a witness said the culprits had Chicago tags."

"I can't save the world, Bee. Drugs ain't going nowhere, brah. I can only do me and save as many as I can," he responded, realizing his limitation.

"I feel you, but if it's true, we definitely don't need them fucking up the city even more. I know we're one of the worst cities in the US, but Chicago—those niggas are on some other shit," he warned.

"I know, but let's not jump to conclusions yet. Let's see how it plays out." Gavin didn't enjoy hearing that news, but he had to keep his plan moving. "You ready to roll, Bee? I need to check on, Cee and the baby, and I need to take Cranberry Vampire to get his shots."

"Fuck you get that name from? Anyway, I'm ready," B-Smoove said, and they headed back to the house.

Ciani was singing to the baby when they walked inside the house. She had lost most of the weight and what remained was lovely. He loved her milk full breast, and her ass was full and thick. She complained about the weight gain, but Gavin wasn't complaining.

"Oh, hey bae, I didn't hear you come in. Hi, Bee," she said changing her tone. "Say hi to daddy lil Gavin," she said, handing him to his father.

"What's up my lil prince," Gavin said and kissed on his forehead. He was only a month old and Gavin was still nervous holding him. He couldn't wait until he grew, so he could spend more time with him. He handed him back to Ciani, and she instantly got an attitude. "What's wrong with you?"

"Nothing!" she spats and took the baby from Gavin. She left him and B-Smoove where they stood and went to her bedroom. Gavin's way of showing love was inadequate and Ciani was holding on by a string.

"Somebody is mad!" B-Smoove said when she left.

"Yea, that's becoming an everyday occurrence."

"Handle your business," B-Smoove said and went into the basement.

Nah, I'll check on my dogs, he thought and went outside to the backyard. He loved training and kicking it with his dogs. The love and loyalty he received from them uplifted his spirit. As soon as they saw him, they went ballistic. He released Cranberry Vampire first before releasing his pit bulls Rebel and Roxy. Admittedly, he favored Cranberry Vampire, and he spent more time training him. However, that day, he kicked it with all of them before locking them back in their cages. He went back inside and Ciani was in the kitchen preparing dinner.

"Why are you mad?" he asked as she banged around the pots and pans, attempting to annoy him.

"Who said I was mad," she said, brushing past him to get the linguini noodles out the cabinet.

"No one had to say shit, Cee. It's clear you got an issue, so just spill it, love."

"If I have to tell you one more time to not call me that, we will have a problem! Save that shit for those bitches that don't know no better!" she retorted.

"What bitches, bae?"

"Any bitch you say it too! I am your wife, but I think you forgot about that—just like you forgot about the marriage license!" She rolled her eyes hard and long.

"We're still on that shit! And, you need to watch your mouth! The cussing is unbecoming!" he warned.

"I don't give a fuck! Sometimes you need to be simple and blunt. I'm sure I'm not going to hell for it!" she replied as she placed the noodles into the boiling water.

"Probably not, but I don't like it, Cee! You're a mother now, so try to refrain from using that language in front of my son!" he advised.

"You should try spending more time with your son! How is he supposed to bond with you if you only hold him for a minute?" she yelled. "And, you know what? I'm tired of this relationship! I lost you after the kidnapping, and you never fully came back! You might disagree, but if you do, you're more delusional than I thought!" she spats.

"Wait, you really believe that, Ciani?" he asked confused by this new vulgar woman standing in front of him. He knew she could get untangled, but this was bullshit.

"Yes, I do! I kept a closed mouth for too long! Between your work and those dogs, me and the baby are coming in last. You may be in denial, but the truth is the truth," she countered.

"Nah, that's your truth, because my love for you have not changed! If anything, it's grown to heights unimaginable!

"Love me less than, because if you love me more, I'm in trouble! But, I'll take responsibility for this situation. I was too quiet for too long!" She stood firm and Gavin was confused, upset, and shocked at her behavior.

"I see you're in feelings, ma but that has nothing to do with me! I'm just trying to spend the rest of my life with you! I'm sorry if you feel as if I'm not spending enough time with you. I never knew it was a problem until now," he said, trying to defend himself.

"It's a problem, Gavin. I withhold a lot of shit I know about you!"

"Like what?" he asked, dying to know.

"Like, you fucking other girls! I don't have physical proof, but I know. Just like I knew you fucked someone when you went to LA!"

"I ain't never cheat on you, Cee and nothing happened in LA! Fuck is you talking about?" he asked nervously, wondering how she knew.

"I can't prove the LA thing, but last week when you came home late, I smelled your dick when you were sleep, and even though you washed that bitch off, I still smelled her!" she yelled. *Fuck, Bishop ain't never lied*, Gavin thought when he remembered what he said about his wife sniffing his balls. He did have sex with an old girlfriend last week and he was unprepared, so he entered her raw, regretting it after. He prayed she didn't get pregnant or have an STD.

"Bae, you're paranoid! I understand women get insecure after giving birth, but you're going overboard," he replied, trying to act as if he was clueless.

"Umm hmm! Listen, I wanted wait until the baby got a little bigger, but I want to go home to Baltimore to visit my father. Since my dad couldn't come visit after the baby, I want to make a trip home," she said, angering him more.

"You should go with your first instincts, babe. The baby is too young to be traveling across country!" Gavin said exaggerating. "Anyway, that's a trip we should take together," he added. He didn't know what she was up to, but he wasn't trusting it. Ciani could be unpredictable, so he decided to keep a watchful eye on her.

"You're right, but as soon as the weather warms up, we out!" she said stirring the noodles.

"That's right, sweetheart! You, me and the baby! We roll as a package deal." She continued with her attitude, refusing to make eye contact with him. "What are you cooking, anyway?" he asked.

"I don't know!" she replied passively.

"What do you mean you don't know? Come on, baby enough with this attitude! I'm not cheating, I love you and only you, and I promise to be more assertive to your needs!" he said, trying to be cool before he snapped. "Well, whatever you're cooking, I know it's gon be good, bae." He tried to lighten the mood because she looked so beautiful even when she was mad as a bull.

"I only made enough for me, because I didn't think you was coming home for dinner," she responded with her lips poked out.

"Damn, you're acting like you hate me! You hate me, Cee?" he asked as he wrapped his arms around her waist. "Ain't no way you gon eat all that pasta by yourself, babe. You that mad that you'll see your husband starve?" he asked as he nibbled on her neck and groped her breath.

"Aaaah!" she bawled, and Gavin thought she was pleased, so he continued. "Stop, Gavin! My nipples are sore from breast feeding!" *Damn*, he thought. "You can't be all rough and tough. These breasts belong to your son for the next nine months.

"Sorry, wife. I'll promise to be gentle, but lil Gavin gon have to share. Are they swollen?" he asked as his nature rose.

"Yes, and heavy. I'm not used to these big ole jolly ranchers," she replied softening her tone.

"Let me see em!" he asked anxiously.

"Okay, but you have to promise you won't touch them," she warned.

"I promise—thugs honor!" he joked, and she laughed for the first time all night. When she was happy, her eyes danced, and Gavin was never left uninspired.

"You so silly! Okay, here goes," she said unbuttoning her

shirt. Gavin got excited because they hadn't made love since the baby. He witnessed her breast feeding many times, but he hadn't seen the new Milky Way's yet. However, he was taken aback when she pulled out bandages from her bra.

"Are your titties bleeding, bae?" he asked confused. "Damn, lil Gavin must be sucking those things raw!"

"They're not bandages, silly! They're breast pads for when my nipples leaks."

"Are they leaking now?"

"No, but they normally leak when Gavin is hungry," she replied as she loosened her bra.

"Damn, babe they're huge and swollen! Can I have some milk?" he asked wanting to suck her firm nipples.

"Eww, no!"

"I want to taste it!" He bent down and gently circled his tongue around her nipple, moving from right to left.

"Yes!" she whispered, and he continued to tantalize her nipples, but he wanted to taste her milk. He sucked softly and was amazed when the breast milk fell into his mouth.

"Umm, you taste so good!" he moaned. It was warm and nasty, but he played it off. However, Gavin didn't realize that Ciani was having difficulties releasing the milk from her breast. The milk began to flow freely from his warm tongue and Gavin started choking. "Yo, this shit is out of control!" he said as he wiped his mouth.

"Wow, thanks honey. I've been trying to get this flow

since I gave birth. Move!" she demanded as she cut off the stove and ran upstairs. Gavin was on her heels, wondering why she left him. He followed her into the room, observing her every move. "Babe, run and get the rest of the bottles out the pot downstairs. I need to load up while I can," she requested. He did what she asked and hurried back.

"Here you go beautiful!" He handed her the bottles and watched her like a hawk. He was slightly amazed, and he knew Ciani would be a great mother. By the time she finished she had filled six three-ounce bottles with milk. She sealed the bottles and told Gavin to place them in the fridge. When he came back, she was completely naked and ripe for the picking. "I've been waiting for this for what felt like forever!" he said and joined her on the bed.

"You got a condom?" she asked.

"Fuck no! Why would I have a condom, Cee?" he asked wondering what her problem was.

"I'm not supposed to have sex for six weeks. The doctors said I could get pregnant right away," she explained.

"I'll pull out, babe," he replied with no intention on strapping Jeffries.

"Yea right!"

"For real," he replied, as he tasted her sweetness. Ciani needed him and he felt so good. She couldn't remember the last time he went downtown, but it was a welcomed gift that day. He took her body to heights she didn't know was possible.

140

"Oh, you know that feels so good!" she yelled, and Gavin enjoyed pleasing her. He couldn't wait to feel her walls against Jeffries.

"You like that?" he asked and went down again. When he came up for air, he stripped quickly. He climbed on top of her body and injected her vagina with his thickness. She felt wonderful to him, even better than he remembered. "We are fucking all day!" he said, meaning every word. He continued to stimulate and obliterate her vagina, taming her mind and sending her into a frenzy. Ciani thought it was the best sex they had. She was overdue for some good loving and he didn't disappoint.

"Turn over," he insisted. When she was in the position, he took a moment to admire her beautiful ass, before mildly slipping inside. "Your pussy is so sweet! I will kill a nigga over it!" he groaned as he dug out her insides.

"Fuck me harder," she demanded, and he obliged. They devoured each other for forty-five minutes until Gavin exploded inside her. "Gavin, I told you I could get pregnant!" she complained.

"Sorry, babe, you just felt so good, and there ain't nothing wrong with having another baby," he said trying to pacify her.

"That's easy for you to say since you're not the one who has to carry it."

"You got me on that one, sweetheart." Gavin Jr cried because it was feeding time.

"Sorry, babe, but duty calls," she said and headed to the nursery to get the baby. She brought him back into the room and Gavin bonded with them both. He enjoyed watching her feed his son, knowing he was getting the best nutrition. After she burped him, Gavin held him until they both feel asleep. Ciani smiled with joy when she saw the baby laying on Gavin's chest. She placed him back in the crib and joined Gavin for some much-needed rest.

For the next two weeks, Gavin was overly supportive and loving towards Ciani and the baby. He spent most of his time getting to know his son and wife again. At the time, Gavin believed all her needs were met.

CHAPTER 15

A month later, the city was alive. For it to be March, the weather was in the low eighties, and the streets were busy. Kids were running wild and ballers were out stunting. Gavin had just received the permits to build his second location. He took Tamika's advice and added females to the roster. The construction was underway, and Tamika already had her list of the first twenty. Everything in Gavin's life was stable, and he was genuinely happy with his family life and businesses. However, Ciani didn't feel the same way. Gavin showered her and the baby with love for two weeks after their make-up love session, but he was slipping back into his old habits. She felt them drifting apart, and she wasn't keen on not being involved with the business. When she mentioned she was ready to come back to work, he suggested she work with his mom and sister running the daycares. Her feelings were brutally hurt. She could remember a time when he needed her as inspiration, but it seemed he found someone or something else to inspire him. He was back to spending hours with his dogs while pacifying Ciani and the baby. For the first time in her adult life, she was at a loss. She didn't know what she would do with her future. She had no desire to be a stay at home wife, and if that's what Gavin desired, they would encounter a serious problem.

She was sitting home, feeling sorry for herself before she called Gavin's phone. "Hey, babe. I hope this isn't a bad time," she said when he answered the phone.

"It's always a good time to hear from you, my world. What's up with my, baby?" he asked.

"I'm going crazy sitting around the house all day. I know we talked about going to Baltimore when the weather broke, and I think it's a good time," she reasoned.

"Nah, bae! Unfortunately, I can't leave right now. Construction is starting on the other building and I need to be here," he replied, and he heard her sigh through the phone.

"You don't have to come since you're so busy. I haven't been home for forever, and I miss my dad," she explained.

"Cee, I already told you we're taking that trip together. Let me look at my calendar and get back to you," he replied, unwilling to hear that bullshit she was talking.

"Yea, you do that, but if you can't find time within the next two weeks, we will leave you!" she warned.

"Listen, don't fuckin threaten me, Cee! I just don't understand what the problem is!"

"I'm not a stay at home wife or mother. I had a fulfilling career before you, and I want to get back in the mix!"

"How will going to Baltimore fix it? That shit don't make no since!" he replied agitated.

"I'm not about to argue with you, but like I said—if you can't find time in two weeks, don't worry about it!" she spats and hung up on him

What the fuck, he thought looking at his phone. He was about to call her back, but Tamika and B-Smoove walked into his office.

"What's up with y'all," he asked when they entered the office.

"Three kids got shot in the crossfire last night. Two are dead and the three-year-old is in critical condition, holding on to her life." Tamika explained, informing him of the deadly incident.

"Damn, how old was the kids that died?" he asked.

"Six and nine!" she replied appalled.

"Yea, my homie lives near the incident, and he said those Chicago thugs are warring with the local small-time dealers. I think these nigga's are trying to pick up where Quadir left off, and take over the city," B-Smoove added.

"Chicago! This is the second time I'm hearing about these muhfucker's—sorry Meek!"

"Oh, I'm not offended, Gavin. I made a few calls, and this situation is about to get bad before it gets better. The police department is aware, but have no true leads because these men aren't local. Until they can lock one up, the investigation is stale," Tamika explained.

"This is some bullshit!" he spat. "It's one thing to deal with the local dealers, but these out-of-town fools is a whole other situation."

"I just wanted you know, big brah! Shit is about to get ugly," B-Smoove said.

"Fuck you talking about, Bee! You ain't getting involved in that shit! Let the cops handle that!" Gavin warned.

"Whatever!" he responded

"Yo, Bee, I'm not fucking around. We need to stay focused on our shit!"

"I hear you."

"You better muhfucker! I know your ass and I'll be watching you."

"Gerald, I think Gavin is right," Tamika agreed calling by him his birth name.

"I'm good, but on another note, two more people volunteered to help with the after-school program. We have forty kids showing up and not enough teachers and tutors," he explained. "And, we're running out of room. Ms. Jones has to hold class in the reception area."

"Forty kids, that's what up! The basement will be finished soon, so we'll have the room we need," he advised.

"Bill called and said he couldn't get you. He sounded disappointed when I told him you weren't here," Tamika said.

"Damn, alright let me call him back real quick. We can

revisit this another day," Gavin said, dismissing them. "Oh, Bee, thanks for sticking around. I'm glad you decided to come and work full-time. I know you had other plans," Gavin said.

"No doubt," he replied, and they left. Gavin called Bill right after.

"Pops, I'm sorry I missed your call. What's up?" Gavin asked.

"Gavin, I need to see you to discuss a personal matter. This can't be done on over the phone, but I was hoping you could make some time next month," he explained.

"Sure, just tell me when and where, and you know I'm there," he replied.

"Thanks son, I'll have my secretary send you the time and place. I'll have a private jet for you, so don't worry about transportation."

"Cool, I'll make sure to check my email."

"Great, how's the program coming along?"

"It's coming along well. Thanks again for everything you did to help me and them."

"It was my pleasure. I'll chat with you soon, son," he said and ended the call.

Gavin wondered what personal matter he was describing, but it didn't matter, because he would be at that meeting. He didn't want to let B-Smoove know that he was concerned with the news. He knew these cats could be problematic for the city and his program. He was trying to pick his battles well, but this shit was falling right into his lap. The news and Bill's call distracted him from Ciani's complaining. However, his mind was back on her and he needed to get to the root of the problem.

CHAPTER 16

Somewhere in Bucks County, Juice was plotting on new territories to take over. When they heard the news that Quadir was dead, Juice sent fifty workers to Philly. There was no love lost over his cousin because Quadir was always out for self. Juice remembered when he first started, he reached out to Quadir trying to lock down a supplier, but he shot him down. They weren't close, so he brushed it off, because they only saw each other at rare family functions.

He received word that Philly was up for the taking. He understood it was risky to try to take a whole city, but he believed it could be accomplished. He needed to touch base with his crew because he remembered specifically telling them to chill until he came. He heard his men were responsible for several deaths including kids. was livid when he found out how sloppy they handled the situation. He always tried to be careful when kids were around, but he knew accidents happened too. His plan was to creep into Philly and catch everyone off-guard. However, news had already spread about Chicago's arrival. He was cool with his uncle's and they put Quadir on, but when he became bigger than life, he turned his back on the entire family. The neighborhood was quiet which he loved because he could keep a low profile. He left his lead workers in charge of Chicago and he was confident they would keep his business booming in his absence. He was meeting his Uncle Chub to find a place for the seventy-five workers that were staying at different hotels around Philadelphia. Juice needed to lock down locations because the hotel bill was about to kill him. He pulled into the parking lot behind Warm Daddy's where he was meeting his uncle. When he walked around to the front door, he was pleasantly surprised to see the place was full of beautiful Philly women. Whoever said Philly girls weren't cute was on some bullshit. He was feeling these women and couldn't wait to take a dip in their ponds.

"Ed, over here." Uncle Chub called him by his birth name when he spotted him inside the restaurant.

"Unc, what's good whatcha! Thanks for meeting me so soon," Juice greeted as he sat down at the table.

"No doubt! Welcome to the City of Brotherly Love. You ready to get this money?" he asked.

"Twenty-four-seven, Unc! But, I need locations for my workers like ASAP. My shipment just came in today, and I'm ready to unleash that shit and flood the streets. I've been told they are loving our shit!" he replied pleased with his information.

"I'm sure they are considering muhfucker's are

scrambling trying to keep their clientele intact. From what I'm hearing on the streets, it's a freefall out there. Pop up corners are happening everywhere, and there's no order or loyalty. Quadir was a menace to society, but I'll give him credit for keeping order among his workers. He ruled by fear and fear alone."

"Speaking of Quadir, what the fuck happened? I mean, I don't see no one trying to avenge him or find out who killed him," Juice wondered.

"His workers hated him and the ones that didn't are dead now. As far as who killed him, everyone knows. Gavin Douglas aka Gavin the Magnificent killed him. The police know too, but they ain't trying to fuck with him, since he almost took down an entire precinct.

"Gavin the Magnificent? Who the fuck names themselves that weak shit!" Juice asked astounded.

"I think that's his bike name, but like you said that is some weak shit!" Uncle Chub agreed.

"So, why is this man still breathing?"

"Listen, Quadir ain't have no loyalty to family. We put him and Gavin on when they were in college. They started pushing small weight to the elite, but when Quadir graduated, they went their separate ways and Quadir took over Philly. From what I know, Gavin wasn't having it. By that time, Quadir built relationships with several suppliers and took the city by storm. When he became bigger than life, he said fuck family and we could never contact this dude," he explained.

"Is that why he wasn't at grandma's funeral?"

"Exactly, my mother raised him and did everything in her power to keep him on the straight and narrow path. However, he shitted on her and the rest of us. After the funeral, I disowned him as my nephew. May his ungrateful sorry ass rest in hell! No one is missing this nigga except the crack heads."

"So, what's up with this Gavin character?" Juice asked curious and wondering if he needed to handle him personally.

"I don't really know, but I think he's like an advocate or some shit! Like a fake Malcom X—you feel me. And, I know he has connections in high places. It's clear someone is watching his back," he replied.

"Oh, okay. As long as he stays out my way, I don't see him being a problem!"

"Nah, you need to be worrying about these Philly thugs! You know we're on the same list as Chicago as far as crime, drugs, and murder. Taking the streets will not easy, so you need to prepare for war, nephew!" he advised.

"I know it won't be a walk in the park, so I'll run through instead!" he replied jokingly.

"Long as you're prepared!" Uncle Chub warned because he knew his nephew may have bit off more than he could chew.

"On a lighter note, I'm trying to get into some Philly pussy tonight! Any suggestions?" he asked.

"Look around—take your pick!" he laughed "But, nah, I got this sweet thing waiting. Do you want me to send her to your spot?"

"Nah, I think I'll get a room at the hotel I saw on the way here." The food came, and Juice enjoyed the cornbread specifically. "Unc, where can I get the best cheesesteak from?"

"For me, the best is Larry's Steaks, but some say Gino's or Pat's are the best. I just happen to disagree with that bullshit! It's according to who you ask," he replied.

"I'm asking you, muhfucker!"

"And, I told you! We can pass by tomorrow if you want."

"Cool, but I want that sweet thing you got waiting!" he said with a wicked smile.

"I got you and I spoke to my friend about the housing. He said he got six apartments available, but they need work. He's willing to do a no lease deal, but he wants six months in advance on all properties," he explained.

"Damn, that's fucking robbery!" Juice spat.

"It is what it is," Unc Chub countered. Later that night, Uncle Chub brought the big butt beauty to his hotel room, and he enjoyed his first night in Philly.

*T*wo weeks later, Juice and his workers were up and running, but the city was back in chaos. Just as Uncle Chub had predicted, the Philly thugs were ready for war over territory. The past week was one of the worse for the city. There were over fifty murders and several casualties. However, the death of a young pregnant mother from an AK-47 sent the city into an uproar. Residents complained and demanded the police do something. It was one thing dealing with the local thugs, but they refused to let these outsiders reign down fear in the city. Once the neighbors found out they were from out of town, voices of anger and frustration surfaced. Particularly, the parents were irate and tired of their children gunned down senselessly in the streets.

Juice was relaxed as he basked in the money his workers made him the last two weeks. The move to Philly proved to be lucrative, and he had no regrets. He watched the news and saw all the complaints, but he was used to that type of negative publicity. Killings ran rampant in Chi-town, so he felt right at home. He wasn't affected by the least.

"Juice, shit is getting hot out there, but we can handle these Philly clowns!" Tone one of his lead workers informed.

"We predicted this shit, but as long as they lay down and we're still standing, let the temperatures rise!" he replied. "I'm feeling the turnover—shit, these zombies been waiting for our arrival! Wayne said they loving our product!"

"No doubt, but you need talk to Wayne. This nigga ain't

taking no chances and just killing anyone who he feels is a threat! The other day this young boy approached him, asking for directions. Instead of telling him he didn't know, he shoots him in the head. Fuck is wrong with dude! We had to leave that location immediately!" he explained.

"You know Wayne is schizophrenic! Leave him alone, I'll talk to him," Juice said, brushing it off. Tone looked at his boss sideways. He wasn't innocent and had his fair share of kills, but he was uncomfortable. The way they came into Philly and took the drug scene by storm, didn't sit well. He knew death or jail was in his near future if he didn't change his situation.

"Juice, we go way back, and I'm telling you that shit wasn't cool! Now, he's bringing in heat from the police!" he warned.

"We know how to handle heat from the cops, Tone. How bout you just focus on collecting the money and leave the other shit to me!" he spats. "Better yet, I need some information on this Gavin character! He killed my cousin and the more I think about it, the more I have a problem. Find that muhfucker!" he demanded.

"I got you, but you never liked your cousin," Tone responded, wondering why his focus shifted.

"Nah, he can rest in hell, but he's still fam, and his murder cannot go unpunished!"

"I'll let you know what I find out," Tone said and left.

Tone had already heard tales about Gavin Douglas and

they were all honorable and noble. He had family in Philly and when he visited, he heard them praising Gavin to no end. His little cousin Diggy appeared to worship him. He decided to keep his knowledge about Gavin and his whereabouts a secret for the moment. He was thirty-six and tired of the hustling game. He believed in God, but his lifestyle kept him from building a relationship due to guilt. Nevertheless, he found himself communicating and praying more often with a desire to be closer to God.

*L*ife was bittersweet for Gavin. The business aspect of life was going as planned, but his personal life was in shambles. Ciani stopped talking to him and he was unable to comfort her. He was exhausted from trying to please her when he didn't know what he did. Nonetheless, he was uneasy about it. He called his mother, needing insight, but she was talking the same babble as Ciani. She suggested he spend more time with her, but he felt like he was doing a great job juggling his business and personal life.

Along with that burden, people were coming to him every day about these Chicago goons. Gavin wanted to get on with his plans, but folks had other plans for him. He sat in office thinking about when he first started hustling and he hated to admit he missed it. He didn't have all this drama, confrontations and love problems. He got in and out, made his money and kept shit moving. It wasn't until Ciani came into his life and erased the old selfish Gavin. Now, the same person who had inspired him, was on the verge of breaking his heart. He was in deep thought when Tamika and Ms. Jones walked into his office.

"Good morning, Gavin!" Ms. Jones greeted.

"Good morning," Tamika added.

"Have a seat and tell me how I can help you!" he replied.

"I was hoping you would consider allowing me to work from the second headquarters with the women," Tamika suggested as she sat down in the chair.

"You trying to leave me already! Am I that bad of employer to work with?" he asked.

"Oh, no, trust me it's not that, Gavin. You know what, forget about it. I can handle both offices from here," Tamika replied, regretting her decision.

"I'm just messing with you, love! I had a feeling this was coming, and I think it's a good idea," Gavin said, wanting her to keep her confidence.

"Oh great! I've been training, Ms. Jones, and she understands the whole system. I feel confident she can pick up where I left off," Tamika assured.

"Yes, I'm ready and you know I would do just about anything for you, Gavin." Ms. Jones said. "Wanda is ready to step into my shoes, so you wouldn't need to hire anyone else."

"You beautiful ladies are so smart and sweet. I'll miss

seeing you, Tamika, but if you can turn the women camp into a success like you did here, I'm for it one hundred percent!"

"Thanks so much for understanding. And, yes I will make that place a success!" she said excited. She couldn't wait to make the move, thrilled to be hands on with the females.

"Here's the bad news, six more kids were shot coming home from school! Thankfully, they're saying they will all make it, but they were caught in the crossfire just like the rest. It's as if Quadir was reincarnated because we haven't seen this type of nonsense since he was alive!" Ms. Jones explained.

"You're absolutely right, Ms. Jones! I think this might be worse though. More innocent kids are becoming victims of this new Cartel, which throws a monkey wrench into our program. Those could've been our kids that come to the after-school program!" Tamika sighed.

They both started at Gavin as if he had the answers and he instantly became tense. He was trying to stay in his lane, but the more he heard about these thugs, the more burning his anger became. The cops appeared to be useless because Gavin thought they would've nipped this shit in the bud. Instead, it appeared they were sitting back allowing the black on black crime as usual.

"What do y'all want me do!" he yelled. "I'm sorry, I didn't mean to raise my voice, but we need to let the cops handle them. Don't get distracted by the news. Just focus on how far we've come," he said, and they agreed by shaking their heads. "I'm about to head out, ladies. I'll talk to y'all later."

When Gavin got inside his car, he heard his untraceable phone ringing. He knew it could only be Silas or Bill. He reached under the seat, retrieved the phone and quickly answered.

"Gavin, what's up my fren?" Silas asked when he answered.

"Chilling, what's up with you? I know it must be something if you're calling this number," Gavin replied.

"You know it! Here's the 411, my man! Edward Spinks, aka Juice is your new Philly kingpin. Oh, and ah, he's Quadir cousin!" he said casually.

"His fucking cousin, what cousin is this because I know most of his peeps?" Gavin asked while his tension built.

"Obviously, his Chicago cousin. I'm just giving you some tea, my man. I hope you reconsider and move out here. Sometimes you need to leave the jungle behind. You can still do great things for your community three thousand miles away, Gavin," he replied in hopes Gavin would reconsider.

"I hear you, but thanks for the information. At least, I know who I'm dealing with and hopefully I can eliminate the problem. Yo, don't tell Annabella, because she'll call, Bill and I don't need that right now."

"My lips are sealed," he said and ended the call. Gavin realized he couldn't leave this to the police and he would have to involve himself.

When he reached home, he didn't recognize the inside of the house because Ciani had redecorated the entire space. It looked beautiful, and it felt real home. He thought that was a good sign, so he was hopeful when he walked into the bedroom.

"Hey, sweetheart! I see you've been busy. The downstairs looks wonderful!" he complimented.

"Thanks," she dully replied. "When you have nothing else to do, you find yourself spending unnecessary money."

"That was money well spent, bae. I love it! Listen, I know you bored and tired of being in the house all day. I was being selfish, wanting you all to myself. But, I think you should go see your dad. I wanted to go with you, but with the new building and everything else, I know I can't leave right now," he said. He was uneasy since the phone call and needed to make sure his family was safe. He believed she would be safer in Baltimore.

"For real, babe. You really mean it!" she brightly replied.

"Yes, so get packed. I'm driving you and the baby down tomorrow."

"I thought you said you couldn't come?" she asked confused.

"I can't stay, but there's no way I'm sending you down there alone. Plus, I want to meet your pops and I'll head back the next day," he explained.

"Thanks, so much, and thanks for sticking around for at least a day!" she responded and began packing immediately.

"You know I always got you!" He kissed her and helped her pack.

When they reached Ciani's father home, Gavin was pleased and felt Ciani would be in a safe and healthy environment. He owned a modest single-family home that was inviting from the outside. The lawn was well kept, and the home looked as if a fresh coat of paint was just applied. He parked on the short driveway that led to the house and her father and new stepmother came outside.

"Ceecee, my sweet little girl!" her father greeted. "I missed you something awful," he said as he hugs her tight and snug, making it hard for her to breathe.

"I missed you too, daddy! she responded, and Gavin saw how happy she was in her father's arm. He was slightly jealous because he had come face-to face with someone who loved her just as much as he did. Her eyes were sparkling, and Gavin thought that gift was reserved for him only.

"You look so beautiful, Ceecee, just like your mother," he said as he stared at her with admiration.

"Daddy, I want you to meet your grandson and your son-in-law. This is Gavin and this little handsome man is, Gavin Junior," Ciani said as she took the baby from Gavin and handed him to her father. "Gavin this is my dad, Roy."

"I'm so happy to finally meet you!" he lied as he extended his hand. "Ciani talks about you all the time. I'm sorry we're just meeting, but hopefully we can spend more time in the future," he said, trying to impress for the sake of Ciani. Roy shook Gavin's hand quickly before placing all the attention on Gavin Jr.

"Oh, look at my beautiful grandson! Let's get you all inside. It's getting a little cold," Roy replied.

"Hello!" his wife said, reminding him she wasn't just a statue.

"Oh, I'm sorry, dear! This is my wife, Sylvia. With all the excitement I forgot she was standing there," he said jokingly.

"It's nice to meet you both, and this baby is stunning, but like your father said, it's getting a little chilly out here. Come inside. I've prepared a wonderful dinner for you!" she added.

When they entered, Gavin and Ciani felt right at home. The smell of Sunday dinner warmed their souls, and they both felt at peace. Gavin began to relax as he prepared himself for Roy.

"So, Gavin, Ciani tells me you do a lot for your community. I know that can be a dangerous job and I hope you're taking measures to keep my daughter safe," he said, but it was more of threat.

"Always, Roy—I mean, you don't mind if I call you that?" he asked.

"Roy is fine. What else do you do outside of helping your people?" he asked.

"I own a few fast food restaurants, daycares, and other investments."

"Well, I tell you this—it is good to know I have a rich son! Sylvia break out that expensive twenty-dollar bottle of wine! Let's celebrate!" he replied, and everyone erupted in laughter.

"I'll take the baby while you guys sit down and eat," Sylvia said. They ate, laughed and enjoyed each other company for the rest of the evening. Gavin and Roy had a lot in common, in that they were silly as bees. Gavin now understood why Ciani appreciated his sense of humor.

"Bae, I don't mean to interrupt your movie, but can you get the baby things out the car," she asked, disturbing Gavin and Roy Marvel Marathon. Once they found out they both loved the Marvel series, Roy pulled out his entire collection.

"Sure, babe—right away!" he replied.

"I'll pause it for you," Roy said when Gavin left.

"Dad, can you help him because it's a lot of stuff? He brought the whole nursery," Ciani laughed.

"Of course, sweetheart!" Ciani felt wonderful, and she knew she would have a great time with her dad and Sylvia. From what Ciani could see, Sylvia wasn't only a great cook, but she was a kind woman. The tension was broken, and everyone got along.

Once Gavin and her dad carried everything in, Sylvia offered to babysit for the night, so they could be alone. Ciani accepted her offer and gave Gavin the fuck of his life. She made sure she left an impression, knowing they would be separated for a few.

The next morning, Sylvia made a breakfast fit for kings. She had waffles, pancakes, grits, eggs, turkey sausage and turkey bacon. Ciani was looking forward to her cooking the next few weeks. After breakfast, Gavin showered and dressed. Ciani was becoming sad knowing he was about to leave her.

"Come here, babe," he demanded, and she obeyed. "Don't get too comfortable down here, because I'll be back to get you a couple of weeks. I hope this time with your family will make you happy. I will miss you and lil Gavin to the moon. I don't know how I will make without you two," he said meaningfully.

"You'll be fine, my king! Anyway, if it becomes too much, I'll come home right away!" she responded soothing his ego.

"Yea!" he grabbed her inside his arms for some final loving and it was hard to break away. "Hey, if you don't know nothing else, know that I love you. I'm about to roll before you get Jeffries excited. I'll call you as soon as I reach home."

"Okay, love you more!" she said and walked him to the door.

"Gavin, it was a pleasure to meet you, son. I hope you don't be a stranger," Roy said as he stood by the door.

"I made you a lunch, so you don't have to stop at those dreadful food stops. There's a turkey sandwich, chips, bottled water, and a few of my famous chocolate chip cookies!" Sylvia said as she handed Gavin the brown paper back. He felt as if he was back in elementary school.

"Thank you so much. Dinner was delicious, and I'll see you when I come to pick up my family," he replied and left. But, before he could open the door, Ciani ran to him and wrapped her arms around his body tightly. "Don't make this harder than it already is, wife. It's hard to let you go even for a couple of weeks," he said as he held her back.

"I'm sorry. I'm just gonna miss your handsome face. Drive safe husband and I'll be waiting for your call," she replied and released him. He gave her peck on the lips and quickly jumped inside the car.

CHAPTER 17

Gavin drove over the speed limit down I95 and made it home in less than two hours. He stopped by his moms to check on her since he hadn't spent much time with her. When he walked into the massive kitchen, he wasn't surprised to see B-Smoove stuffing his face.

"What's up greedy?" Gavin greeted and sat down at the island next to him.

"Nuttin, you got Cee down there safe and sound?" he asked, continuing to eat.

"Yea, she's good. Where's mommy?"

"She just left with Garin. I'm surprised you didn't see her when you came in," he replied.

"Damn, I wanted to talk to her about something!" he said disappointed she wasn't there. "Listen, Silas gave me the scoop on our little guest. He's Quadir's cousin, which is a problem. We need to deal with this ASAP!" Gavin explained.

"You damn right we do!" he replied ready to protect his brother. "Do you know where he's residing?"

"Nah, but hopefully I'll get that information soon. I need

the word to go out that we're looking for Juice ass! Call Bishop and Pop and find out what they're hearing. Also, hire armed security guards at both headquarters. Did they install the cameras yet?" Gavin asked, taking the necessary precautions.

"Nah, but I'm on it. Listen, I was talking to mommy, and she suggested I stay with her and Kirk when Ciani get back. I know she's tired of me. Garin is moving back to Philly, but it's not like mommy don't have the room. She's in love with this five-bedroom house. I told her I would only stay until I found somewhere permanently."

"As long as she's cool, I'm good. You ready to leave?"

"Yea, let me grab some aluminum foil, so I can take this with me," he replied, and Gavin just shook his head.

Gavin stopped at the women's building because he wanted to let Tamika and the staff know to be careful. He was making provisions to protect his buildings, but he wanted them to be aware of their surroundings. He was pleased when he walked inside. The décor was much different from his other building and It was obvious this location was for the women. The walls were light pink with flowers and candles strategically placed throughout the lobby. This pleased Gavin and he approved of the ambiance.

Before he went to see Tamika, him and B-Smoove peeked in the classroom and all the young women were engaged. One of the ladies spotted him and said, "Good afternoon, Mr. Douglas and thanks for the program!" she yelled. The women turned around and everyone greeted Gavin, making him feel like a celebrity.

"You don't have to thank me, love, just make me proud—you feel me!" he replied.

"Oh, we will!" Another shouted.

"That's what up! I won't interrupt your session any longer. What's your name, love?" Gavin asked the woman teaching the class.

"Me, oh I'm Mrs. Claire and I teach an array of classes," she replied.

"Welcome onboard, Mrs. Claire! It was nice meeting you all," he said, and they headed to Tamika's office. "Hey, beautiful, how's your day?" he asked when they entered her office.

"Gavin, what a surprise! My day is going great, but since I've been working for you, all my days are wonderful!" she replied smiling. She loved what she was doing, and she appreciated her job. Gavin was the best employer she ever had, and he always took her seriously.

"I'm glad to hear that! I just stopped by to let you know I'm hiring security guards and they will be armed. I need to secure both locations. Also, I need to you watch your surroundings always. Until I feel safe, you and the staff will be escorted to your cars after business hours," he explained.

"Is everything okay?" she asked concerned.

"You don't have to worry, I'll protect you!" B-Smoove interjected.

"We're good, but I'm just making sure my employees are safe and sound."

"Okay, I'll inform the staff that we'll have some additions," she replied.

"I'll come every night to make sure you get home safe, Ms. Tamika. By the way, are you married?" B-Smoove asked pushing the envelope.

"Yea, she's happily married, Bee! Stop trying to push up on my best employee!" Gavin warned.

"Your husband is a lucky man, beautiful!" B-Smoove said.

"Thank so much!" she replied flattered.

"Alright, I won't take up any more of your time. One last thing, you need to contact that temporary employment agency I used before. See if the lady is still willing to hire my peeps. I think that will be a great resource for the women getting immediate employment."

"I spoke to her already, and she's onboard. I got you, lol!" she said, because he always said that to her.

"Cool! Let's roll, Bee," he said, and they headed to other building.

For the next two weeks, Gavin was scrambling trying to find Juice location. The shootings continued but thankfully, no more murders were reported in the past few days. Gavin was uneasy knowing Juice wanted him dead. He needed to find him before it was too late. However, the information he needed had fallen into his lap. When he arrived at work, he was happy to see one his favorites, Diggy though he didn't recognize the man that accompanied him. When Diggy saw him come in, he immediately stood with confidence and shook Gavin's hand. Teaching them to be assertive was mandatory from all teachers. When they left the program, Gavin wanted them to be self-aware and self-confident. He was proud of Diggy. He was graduating soon and heading to college. Gavin paid for the entire prom and all his graduation fees. Tamika was able to get him a few scholarships and Gavin funded the balance.

"Hey, Mr. Gee, I was hoping you had a moment to talk to me?" Diggy asked. Although, he told them they could call him by his first name, Diggy never felt comfortable, so he continued to respect him.

"I always got time for you, Diggy!" Gavin replied as he placed his hand on his shoulder. "What can I do for you, do you need more stuff for graduation?" he asked.

"Nah, you took care of everything. Thanks again and mom told me to tell you thank you too!"

"No problem, who's your friend?" Gavin asked wondering who the unknown man was. Bishop, Pop, B-Smoove and Sharif eyes stayed glue to the man, which eased Gavin mind. He trusted each of them.

"This is my, Uncle Tone. He wanted to meet you," Diggy said, holding his head down.

"Fuck you holding your head down for? Lift that shit up—you know better, Dig!" Gavin spats and Tone watched the interaction closely. It was clear that Gavin had his nephew best interest, and he was feeling better about his decision.

"I'm sorry, Mr. Gee. I didn't really want to bother you," Diggy replied.

"It's cool youngin! Tone, you want to follow me to my office. Diggy, you can wait here," he said and Bishop, B-Smoove, Sharif and Pops followed them. They were on Tone's back, but he was used to being in uncomfortable situations. "So, how can I help you?" Gavin asked when they entered his office.

"I'm no snitch, but my boss, Juice wants you dead! He gave me orders to find you and report back. When we came to Philly, I thought we would set up shop and keep shit on the low. But, Juice has other plans, and now he wants to avenge a nigga that never checked for him!" Tone explained.

"Quadir?" Gavin asked.

"Bingo! But, what's fucked up is Quadir never even acknowledged this nigga! When he reached out for assistance with a connect, Quadir acted like he didn't know Juice. Anyway, for the short time I've been in this city, I only hear good things about you. I'm leaving the game and after today, I won't be able to go back to Chicago. I was hoping in exchange for Juice whereabouts, you might have a job for me. My nephew can't stop saying good shit about you!" Tone explained.

"How the fuck we know we can trust you!" B-Smoove snapped. He was tired of people coming for his big brother and he didn't trust Tone. "Matter fact, how we know your whole team ain't hiding around a corner or some shit!" he continued.

"I understand your concerns. Shit, I wouldn't trust me, but all I have is my word. I'm not onboard with selling drugs or killing innocent people over that shit. Actually, I'm trying to get closer to God. It's time for a nigga to repent for his sins and make a change. I'm willing to put in work and start at the bottom," he said. Tone had money saved, but he wanted to make sure he had a steady stream of income coming in each month, preferably from legitimate employment.

"Tone, you definitely caught me off guard! I wasn't expecting this shit, but I know all about, Juice aka Edward Spinks!" Gavin said, letting him know he was already informed. "You have to excuse my brother, because we don't trust many, but if you produce this fool, I'll see what I can do about adding you to the payroll," Gavin said and B-Smoove shot him an irate look. He was ready to put a bullet in Tone's head.

"Thanks, that's all I ask," he replied.

"So, where is this nigga?" Gavin asked.

"He's renting a house out in Bucks County. Here's the address," Tone said as he handed Gavin a piece a paper with Juice's location.

"Okay, Tone if this information is correct, I'll add you

to the payroll on a trial basis. I mean, you turning on your manz, so we already know you ain't loyal. Don't get me wrong, I appreciate the info, but we don't know you from a can paint."

"Right!" B-Smoove concurred.

"Nah, I've been loyal to the devil, but my allegiance has changed and I'm choosing salvation over hoes and bro's— you feel me!" he responded, meaning every word.

"Okay, we'll see, but don't get mad if you don't receive a welcoming. You can start tomorrow, but you will have to prove yourself," Gavin explained.

"No doubt, whatever you need," Tone replied relieved that Gavin was receptive to his concerns. "Oh, before I forget, his worker Wayne is the one responsible for all the deaths. You would need to handle him too because they're like brothers. He hustles around 60th and Dicks on the south side," he continued.

"Alright, my man thanks again for the info, and I'll see you tomorrow around nine," Gavin said dismissing him.

"I'll be here!" he said before joining Diggy.

"Sharif, watch that nigga!" Gavin instructed.

"I'm already on it!" Sharif replied and quickly left so he could tail Tone.

"How you wanna handle, Juice?" B-Smoove asked when everyone left.

"There's only one way to handle him! However, he's won't die by our hands," Gavin responded.

"What's the plan?"

"I want to keep this as quiet as possible. Me, you, Bishop and Pops can handle this shit!"

*L*ater that night, they scoped Juice's location and waited for the perfect time to make their move. They watched the house for an hour before they saw several hoes leaving. Gavin knew they were paid thots by the way they carried themselves. The house had a one-car garage, which was perfect for what they were trying to do. They drove Bishop's blue van, but Gavin changed the plates on it, taking extra precautions.

"Yo, we should snatch his ass as soon as the women drive off!" Bishop suggested.

"We need to make sure he's alone. We're walking in and out alive—you feel me," Gavin said, trying to calm B-Smoove down. He knew his brother was amped.

"We can sit out here all night, or we can do what we came to do," Pop added.

"Alright, pull up in front of this house right here," Gavin instructed, and Bishop obeyed. The neighborhood was quiet, but that could be a problem. Gavin knew the quiet ones had the newsiest neighbors. "Me and Bee will go around the back. When you see the garage doors open, drive in quick," Gavin instructed. They snuck around the back of the house

174

and It was dark, but B-Smoove was quick and efficient with picking the locks. Luckily, for them, no alarm went off, and they found themselves inside the kitchen. "Shhhh!" Gavin said as they crept into the living room.

"Wait!" B-Smoove said when he heard someone coming down the stairs. Juice was clueless and ran straight into death. He hadn't experienced a foursome in a longtime and he was still wheeling from the women. However, when he was greeted with B-Smoove gun, he knew he would never experience a foursome again.

"I heard you were looking for me!" Gavin said and B-Smoove hit him hard across his face with the gun. Blood spewed from his forehead and B-Smoove followed it with a knee to the gut.

"Open the Garage!" B-Smoove insisted. "This nigga ain't going nowhere."

Gavin opened the garage and Bishop drove inside. B-Smoove found some rope inside the garage and quickly restrained him. Gavin shoved him into the van and they drove away quickly. Gavin took him back to the bike club. After Quadir death, Gavin had it renovated, and it was almost complete.

Juice lost consciousness from all the blood loss, but he came around just in time. B-Smoove dragged him out the van and they quickly forced him inside the building. Juice had a feeling who was responsible for his capture and he was thinking if they let him live, he would kill Tone and his entire family. He knew Wayne and his uncle would never deceive him, so it had to be Tone.

"You can tell that bitch ass, Tone that his days are numbered. When I don't show up, they will be looking for him," Juice said as he tried to regain his senses.

"Don't nobody give a fuck! Your first mistake was coming to Philly thinking you could run shit, but the second and most deadly mistake was targeting my brother! Fuck you thought, you were just gonna come and niggas was just gon bow down!" B-Smoove taunted. "Nah, you fucked with the wrong city, bitch!" B-Smoove socked him in the face again.

"Hold up, let me get this," Gavin said and answered his phone. "What's up Sharif?" he asked.

"I followed dude like you asked, and he's staying with the young boy and his family," he replied.

"You mean, Diggy?"

"Yea, and so far, he seems like he was telling the truth."

"Good, bring him to the bike club. Let him know I want to see him about that job," Gavin instructed, and Juice stared at him with hate and humiliation. "Bee, get something to put under him. I'm not trying to get the floors done again!" he instructed.

*T*hirty minutes later, Sharif arrived with Tone by his side. Juice intuition was proven when he saw Tone rolling with Gavin's counterpart. "You snake muhfucker!" He yelled.

"Your ass can never go back home, bitch! You think you're safe after they kill me?" he asked. "Nah, nigga Chicago will come for you!" he said as if he was the Pope.

"Fuck Chicago!" Gavin retorted. "And, for your information, we're not going to kill you," he said, and Juice had hope for a second. "Nah, I'll give ya boy, Tone that privilege!"

"You packing?" B-Smoove asked Tone.

"Yea," he replied dully. He knew he would have to kill Juice to prove himself to Gavin, but he was willing to take that L. He wasted no time pulling out his gun and shooting juice in the head.

"Damn, I wasn't ready for that shit! You caught me off guard, nigga! B-Smoove said impressed.

"I hope that proves my loyalty and I hope I'm not tested this way again. I told you before I'm trying to build a relationship with God!" He was somewhat agitated because he never had a desire to kill Juice. He didn't agree with his tactics, but they had some good history together.

"I think you're good, money. And, to show you that I'm loyal, I'm going to make you head of security for my two headquarters. Sorry, we had to pull you away from what you were doing, but I think we're all good now!" Gavin reassured. "One last thing, we need to take care of your friend Wayne. I need a picture, a location, and we'll handle the rest." Tone pulled up Juice Instagram account, took a screen shot, and sent it to Gavin's phone. "Thanks Tone! Sharif will take you back home." Gavin said.

"No doubt!" he responded, and they left.

"So, what are we doing with the body—same as Shy?" Bishop asked.

"Nah, leave his ass on the streets, so his punk ass workers can see! It's time for them to say farewell to Philly!"

"What about that nigga Wayne, we handling him too?" Pop asked ready to pop off. Gavin paid them well and provided health insurance for everyone. Gavin had his loyalty and friendship, so whatever he needed he was riding.

"Nah, Bishop I need you to call Bam and set up a meeting ASAP!"

CHAPTER 18

After Gavin met with Bam, Wayne and several of his counterparts ended up dead. Bam came through and Gavin paid him well. He added him to his payroll for those special jobs he may need in the future. Bam had come up. Not only did he have a beautiful lady by his side, but he had money to care for her needs. Kim and Bam opened a unisex salon in Camden, New Jersey and business was great. It was a win-win for him, and he accomplished his goal because Kim was in love. Bam turned her pussy upside down and she was so thankful.

Gavin stopped by his second location because he needed to speak with Tamika. She wasn't answering her office phone, and he wanted to know how the program was coming along. As soon as he walked inside, the fruity smell calmed his spirit. He went to her office, but she wasn't there. He made himself at home and made a few calls. Once he wrapped up his last call, he noticed a bag of marijuana on the floor beside her desk. He picked it up, and it was filled with high-grade weed. The potent smell seeped through the bag. Gavin wasn't an expert because he didn't juggle weed, but he knew it was a good product.

"Oh, hey, Gavin. I wasn't expecting you. Is everything okay?" she asked.

"I'm not sure, love. I tried to call you but got no answer, so I stopped by," he replied.

"Well, it's always good to see you! How can I assist?" she eagerly asked.

"First, I need you to explain this!" he said showing her the bag of chronic.

"Uh, I can explain that," she replied shamed and embarrassed.

"I hope so, love because I can't have drugs on the premises!" he warned.

"I know! Normally, I'm more careful and trust me, this won't happen again!" she assured.

"You're a former congresswoman. Fuck you doing running around getting lit for?" he asked, needing a better explanation.

"It's not like that, Gavin. Two years ago, I was diagnosed with Glaucoma! Initially, the doctor prescribed eye drops to use daily, but after six months, my eyes worsened. I was depressed, thinking I was going blind, until I did some research online. That's when I found out that Cannabis was a great treatment for my impairment!" she explained, and she had his full attention. "There were many positive reviews, so I figured I had nothing to lose. My husband is a neuro-surgeon, and he prescribed medical marijuana a few times, but I didn't want him to jeopardize his job and morals. I started copping my own weed and my eyes have remained the same. There's no cure for Glaucoma and it will lead to blindness, but the weed sustains my eyes," she explained, providing a full explanation. She knew she was fired at that point.

"Damn, I didn't know that disease was so severe! Hey, if the weed is working—do you! I won't judge you because we definitely need your eyes, but you can't bring that into the workplace, love!" he replied, softening his intentions to fire her.

"Trust me, it will never happen again! It must have fallen out my bag because I was looking for the weed. I'm so sorry and embarrassed, and I understand if you want to fire me!" she replied, hoping that wasn't her fate.

"Nah, love you ain't going nowhere. Your explanation is good enough for me, just be careful." He cautioned.

"I promise I will and thanks for not firing me!" she replied relieved.

"No doubt! I came to see how the program was coming along, but from what I can see, you got everything under control."

"It is, Gavin! Everything is going great! We just secured five jobs for the women and we added another class. Starting next week, we'll offer support and assistance for pregnant mothers and Post-Partum Depression for mothers after giving birth," she explained proud of her accomplishments.

"Post-Partum Depression? There's a name for it and what does it involve?" he asked, wondering if Ciani was a victim of this disorder.

"Yes, there's a name and it can be a real problem. Specifically, for independent or single women who has no support system. Besides joy, a baby can bring confusion, regrets, anxiety and a whole host of other symptoms. We want women to know that we got them, and we understand," she proudly explained.

"That's funny you mention this because I think my wife may be suffering with these symptoms," he said, hoping she could provide additional insight.

"What kinds of things is she saying or doing?"

"She says I've changed, I'm not supportive, she's bored, she wants to work, and anything else, given the time of day!" he jokingly replied.

"Those are all valid emotions, Gavin. As far as her wanting to work, I think you should let her. From what Ms. Jones and Wanda has told me, she was very influential in handling the headquarters. Honestly, I'm doing her job and she may feel left out," she explained. "I have a great idea! Why don't let you let her run the men's building? Although Ms. Jones got my back, I still do a lot to keep that running properly. Let her take that over and I guarantee, you'll see a change. Some issues are easier than others to resolve."

"You know what, I think you're right, pretty lady! I'll ask her to come back to work because when she was by my side, I was happier and more progressive. Thanks for the talk, Meek! You may have solved my wife problems," he said grateful for the vision.

"No problem, and again, thanks for letting me stay!"

"You can have your desk back! I need to bounce! Talk to you soon," he said and left.

Speaking of Ciani when Gavin left he remembered he was supposed to pick her up from yesterday. He hadn't spoken to her in a couple of days and when he checked his phone, there were no missed calls. *That's strange*, he thought because she always checked in. However, a few minutes later, she called back.

"Hey, bae sorry I missed your call, but I was helping my dad's church with some paperwork," she explained.

"Where's lil Gavin?" he asked, wondering who was watching him.

"He's right here with me. I just fed him and he's about to go to sleep."

"That's good. I'll be there tomorrow to pick you up," he said, missing his wife and child.

"That's what I wanted to talk to you about. I think I want to stick around a little while longer," she said, and Gavin instantly became tensed.

"You already stayed an extra week, and It's time to come home," he said calmly, holding his tongue.

"I know, but I found a job that will allow me to bring Gavin to work," she reasoned.

"What the fuck! Oh, I see what this bullshit is about! You tripping about the marriage license-right?" he asked, because he could never figure out what her problem was. He honestly didn't have a fucking clue.

"Gavin, you don't make time for me or the baby and I can't compete with your passion to save the world!" she countered. "I don't know where I fit into your life, so I think it's best I stay here. I'll come to visit often," she said, continuing to anger him.

"I'm not tryna hear that shit!" he barked and ended the call.

After he hung up on Ciani, she cried, wondering if she made the right decision. She felt safe and loved with her father and Sylvia and she hadn't experienced that in a while. She attended church services again, building her relationship with God and helping the church with paperwork. She felt needed, and she was comfortable living in Baltimore. She was hurt he hung up on her, leaving her hanging, so she decided to give him some time to calm down before calling back.

Later that evening, she indulged in the leftover lasagna from the night before. Sylvia was an excellent cook, and she looked forward to her meals. Sylvia had just rocked lil Gavin to sleep, and he was growing so fast. He was three months, sleeping less and more active. Ciani loved staring at his chubby face. Especially, his eyes because they were the same as hers. Other than that, she believed he looked just like his dad. The doorbell rang, and Sylvia was about to place Gavin in his playpen, but Ciani stopped her.

"Don't get up, I'll get it Sylvia," Ciani offered and when she opened the door, Gavin was standing there with an angry expression. "Gavin!" she yelled surprised.

"Yea, it's me! I came to take you home. I know you haven't been happy since giving birth, but there's no way you're staying here! You and lil Gavin needs to be with me," he replied, unwilling to compromise. "You gon let in or what?" he asked.

"Of course!" she said and allowed him to pass.

"It's good to see you again, Sylvia," he greeted and gently grabbed his son. "Hey little man, daddy missed you and mommy!" he said as he cuddled him in his arms.

"It's good to see you too! Are you hungry, Gavin because we have some leftover lasagna?" she asked.

"Thanks, but I already ate. I just came to swoop up my family real quick," he replied, letting her know he was a quick visit. Ciani didn't inform her dad or Sylvia about her plans to stay, so they had no idea.

"Okay, well I'll start packing the baby things. His clothes are in the dryer. I'll be right back." She left and went into the basement.

"Gavin, I'm not happy in Philly!" she blurted when Sylvia left. "I have no support and since your mother went back to work, I have no one to encourage or talk to. I've felt so alone, but down here, I feel loved and appreciated," she explained.

"I love you more than anyone, Cee and I'm sorry I made you feel that way! That was never my intentions, bae. I promise all that will change when we get home," he replied, attempting to convince her.

"You said that before, Gavin and it didn't last for long! I don't bring nothing to the table anymore," she sighed feeling sorry for herself.

"Cee, you bring everything to my life! I don't know how to function without my sweet wife! Listen, I've been thinking, and I want you to come back to work. It'll be like old times and everyone will be happy," he suggested. "Trying to run from me will never work, bae. I'll go to the ends of the earth to find you."

"Gavin, if you really mean it, I would love to work with you again!" she replied brightly.

"Good! Now, let's get you packed so we can bounce."

"Okay, but I want to wait for my dad to get home before we leave. He will be disappointed if I'm not here when he gets in."

"Whatever you want, bae!" he replied satisfied.

When Roy came home, he was sad to discover his lovely daughter was leaving. He enjoyed her company and bonding with his grandson, wishing she could've stayed longer. Before they said they goodbyes, they promised to visit each other more often. Gavin was anxious to leave before Ciani changed her mind. He quickly got on the road and headed back to Philly.

CHAPTER 19

*T*wo days later, Gavin was content and Ciani was happy, knowing she would be starting work soon. He was getting her office finished and asked them to put a rush on it. He was having a crib and playpen added and he wanted to make sure she had everything needed to perform well. He was on his way home when he heard his phone vibrating. He glanced at his phone and saw it was Annabella.

"What's good Anna! I'm surprised to receive a call from you," he said when he answered.

"I know, but I didn't have a choice in the matter. Bill has been trying to contact you all week!" She said it like he was being scolded. Gavin reached under his seat and grabbed his other phone. He had over twenty missed calls from Bill. He always forgot about that phone.

"Damn, I see he called over twenty times. Let me call him real quick," Gavin said, knowing something was wrong.

"Gavin, that's not possible. Bill died last night!"

"Wa, what did you just say?" he asked, hoping he misunderstood.

"He's gone, Gavin! Bill had Prostate Cancer. He was in remission for several years, but he found out a month ago that the cancer had spread to his brain," she explained and before Gavin could respond, a tear dropped from his eye. He was in shock and couldn't believe the words coming from Annabella.

"Oh my, God, what the fuck man!" he barked and the more he thought about his heart saddened and the tears just flowed. He needed to get a grip, but for some reason he couldn't control the tears.

"I'm sorry it had to be me, but it is what it is! Personally, I'm devastated! Bill and I have a long history and he was a wonderful employer," she said, and Gavin heard her voice crack. "Nevertheless, your presence is required tomorrow afternoon, for the reading of the will. Bill didn't want a funeral, so his family is cremating him.

"What does his will have to do with me?" Gavin asked as he wiped his tears and regained his composure.

"Obviously, you're in it, Gavin! This will be interesting. His private jet will be waiting to fly you to Miami tomorrow. I'll be there to pick you up from the airport," she advised. "And Salas sends his condolences as well," she explained

"But, I don't understand!" he replied still in shock.

"What part, Gavin because everyone knew how Bill felt about you! Again, I'm sorry and I'll see you tomorrow," she said and ended the call. Gavin was spaced out and by the time he reached his house, he didn't remember making it home.

"Hey, handsome husband! How was your day?" Ciani asked when Gavin walked inside. She was playing with the little Gavin with his baby gym. "What's wrong?" she asked when he didn't respond.

"I just found out Bill died last night!" he said as the tears welled in his eyes.

"Oh my, God, baby I'm so sorry!" she said and rushed to his aid.

"I didn't even know he was sick. Annabella said he had Prostate Cancer and it spread. I don't understand why he would keep that away from me!" he sighed and Ciani held him tight.

"Baby, some people don't like to lay their burdens on others, but I understand why you feel in the dark," she comforted.

"I have to fly to Miami in the morning. Annabella said I needed to be there for the reading of the will," he explained.

"Reading of the will, what does that have to do with you?" she asked.

"That's what I said! Anyway, I have to leave early."

"Do you want me to come with you—anything I can do," she responded letting him know she had his back.

"Would you, babe! That would be great because I don't know what the fuck is going on!" he barked.

"Gavin, we'll get through this together like everything else we do. Whatever you need, I got you, boo!"

"Thanks, Cee! I'm blessed to have you in my corner and I'm grateful you came back home. I have a migraine, babe I'm going to take two aspirins and call it a night."

"Okay, I'll pack our clothes and call your mom or Garin to see if they can watch the baby. Go rest and I'll be up shortly."

*T*he next morning, Gavin and Ciani flew to Miami and Annabella was waiting as promised. "Hello, Gavin, I'm so sorry! It's good to see you again Ciani," she greeted.

"Same here," Ciani replied.

"Let's get out of here!" she insisted, and they hopped into the limousine that was waiting.

"Gavin, I need to warn you! The reading of the will may turn deadly! When you have millions of dollars at stake, people will show you their true colors. Bill's attorney is prepared and hired security for this reading," she cautioned.

"Honestly, I'm still confused why I'm even involved. I know Bill cared for me, but I never expected this," he replied uneasy.

"I don't know when or if you will ever recognize the love he had for you. You say you're confused, but everyone in Bill's life including his attorneys knows how much he revered you," she said, trying to explain. "Gavin, you'll be fine in time, but I need you to get your mind right," she continued.

"I hope I don't have a problem with his family because I never asked for this shit!" he responded.

"Just calm down, babe until we hear what they have to say," Ciani encouraged.

"You're right, sweetheart!" he said and fifteen minutes later, they pulled into the attorney's parking lot.

"Okay, we're here. I can't go in with you, but I'll be waiting right here when you get back," Annabella assured.

Bill's attorney greeted Gavin and Ciani and led them to a conference room. When they entered, Gavin spotted his Bill's wife and son. He recognized Bill's wife from the picture in his office, but Bill never talked about her. She was half his age and her face revealed she was anxious to see what Bill left her. Gavin met Bill's son Jasper one time before, but he looked much different from what Gavin remembered. He had a slew of anti-Semitic and white supremacy tattoos covering his body. But, what was most disturbing was the tattoo of the confederate flag on his neck.

"What the fuck are they doing here?" Jasper barked.

"They're here because this is what your father wanted!" Bill's lawyer Coby replied. "Now that we're all here, we can get on with it!" Jasper threw daggers at Gavin and Gavin was ready to fuck him up. He wasn't in the mood for this racist and now he understood why Bill was embarrassed of his son.

"My father was a prick and nigger lover!" Jasper spats.

"Call me a nigger again, bitch!" Gavin warned. Ciani was getting nervous because she could feel Gavin's temperature rise. The three security guards crowded the table when they saw the situation escalating.

"Let's get on with it!" Coby said as he laid the paperwork on the table. After he read the legal statements, he started reading the will. To my wife, I leave you the condo in Miami and twenty million dollars!" Her face lit up and she had a difficult time covering up her joy. "To my son jasper, I leave you fifty million dollars!" Jasper smiled and appeared to be satisfied until he heard what Gavin received. "To my son, Gavin, I leave you five-hundred million, my home in Pennsylvania, Beverly Hills, and Colorado Springs," Coby said, but couldn't finish the rest of statement.

"This nigger is not his son and damn sure ain't no fucking brother of mines!" Jasper barked and leaped across the table. Security wasn't quick enough, but Gavin greeted him with a deadly punch to the temple.

"I will fuck you up, Jasper!" Gavin said and punched him again before security broke them up. He lost all respect and tolerance after his rants and racial comments.

"I swear I will fight this in court! The brain cancer must have altered his decision making!" Jasper protested. "Dad, if you can hear me, I hope you go straight to hell, coon lover!" he continued.

"I agree with Jasper!" Bill's wife concurred. A minute ago, she was the happiest woman on the planet and it was clear neither knew Bill's net worth. Gavin was ready to bounce before he killed Bill's racist son.

"You all have that right, but Bill's wishing is clear. He changed his will a year ago, before the cancer spread," Bill's lawyer explained. "In other words, this will, is air tight, and Bill was in his right state of mind!"

"Fuck this shit! I'll see you all in court," Jasper barked, and security escorted him out the room.

"If you don't have any more questions, Mrs. Kline, you can be excused," Bill's attorney suggested, because he didn't finish reading the will. Also, he had a video Bill made for Gavin and he had to show him before Gavin left.

"Thank you, but this isn't fair and I'm not sure what my husband was thinking! He was fond of you, Gavin, but this is just a slap in the face!" she replied. She grabbed her Chanel purse and left.

"I'm sorry about that!" he said when they left.

"I didn't ask for this shit! So, they need to leave me the fuck alone!" Gavin spats and Ciani comforted him.

"Calm down, baby! It's over now," she encouraged. She was coochie was throbbing and she was ready to take him back to the hotel. After he damn near knocked out, she was horny.

"Not quite, dear. We were interrupted before I could finish. Along with money, you inherited his Bentley and his private Jet. He made this video right before he died. I'll give you some privacy to view the tape. Once you're done, I'll be in my office, just let my receptionist know."

"Thanks," Gavin replied. He was anxious to hear what Bill had to say. His Lawyer opened his laptop, pulled up the video, and left the room. When the video came on Bill lay in a hospital bed, but he looked good. Gavin perked up and gave Bill his undivided attention. Ciani, was curious too, and still trying to absorb the amount of money he inherited.

Well son, if you're watching this than you know I'm gone! Don't mourn over my death, Gavin. I lived a great wonderful full life! From the first time we did business together, I knew there was something special about you. Over the years, I watched you grow into a wonderful man who would make any father proud. Your love for your community and those less fortunate, changed my view on the world. For years, for me, it was always about the money. However, you son, you were a breath of fresh air. You inspire me and I wish I was more like you when I was alive. Nonetheless, I know you will do great things for your community and those that society ruled out. This is why I left my fortune to you. You were rich before, but now you're wealthy and I know you won't abuse this gift. Sure, folks will be upset, but like you always say… I got you, Gavin! Do great things, son and take care of your beautiful wife. Ciani is your match and her passion will sustain you. Take care of my grandson and I'm sorry I never met the little guy, but I know he will have a healthy and happy life. I won't be there to protect you from your bad decision, so I will encourage you to make better ones in the future. However, if you find yourself in a sticky situation, contact Coby, my best friend Steven, and Annabella. I've forgiven her and realized she wasn't fully to blame for what happened to you. You played a role in that situation. Nevertheless, they have your back, but hopefully you'll stay out of trouble. I consolidated your stocks in the business and set up a trust fund for the baby. I don't want you involved with my business partners—those wicked bastards! You have enough money for a lifetime, Gavin. Do your own thing! It's time to say goodbye, Gavin, but before I go, I want you to know that I loved you very much... I hope you know that! Peace Bitch!

The video ended, and Gavin had a difficult time holding in his pain. However, he had to be strong, so he sucked it up and wrapped up his meeting with the attorney. When they reached the hotel, Ciani heart went out to Gavin, and she was sad that Bill died. He gave her plenty of money for the non-profit group she worked for and he always treated her like a queen when she was in his presence.

"Babe, I'm so sorry again! I know today was hard, but you will get through this. Allah will get you through!" she said, attempting to comfort his heart.

"Yea, He will! You are so beautiful, and I'm sorry for ever neglecting you and making you feel sad. Life is short, so I'm going to spend it loving my wife and my life. It's gon take time to get over Bill! Shit, I still can't believe it, but the video helped. It confirmed I'm doing the right thing and plan on making him proud!" he replied.

"Babe, what you gon do with all that money? I mean, if I was his son I'd be mad too!"

"I know, but that pussy was about to join his father! You noticed they didn't get mad until they heard my amount. They were good until the lawyer got to me!"

"Yea, but when he got to you, I thought I'd faint. Five hundred million, Gavin, my goodness!"

"I know I couldn't believe that shit! But, look on the bright side, we can help so many more!"

"You ain't never lied about that, bae!" she sat on his lap and kissed him passionately. Minutes later, Ciani got her wish and Gavin waxed that ass.

CONCLUSION

A few weeks later, everything settled down and Gavin was feeling a little better. He struggled the first two weeks with Bill's death, but the saying, time heals all wounds were true. However, just as Bill warned, the vultures sought out Gavin. He received calls from several moguls, wanting to do business with him. Gavin stopped taking their calls, because he already had his hands full, and what they were offering, he wasn't buying. He didn't need them, so he focused on businesses.

Ciani was back at work and enjoying life again. Gavin realized he should've had brought her back sooner, because Tamika didn't have shit on Ciani. Within a week, she locked down five new sponsors with more to come. When it came to raising money, there was no one like her. Gavin remembered her hustle from the first time he met her on the yacht. Her caring heart was like a magnet and he was blessed to have her up and running again.

Gavin promoted all his friends, including Rich, Bam and Tone. He had his dream team and though loyalty wasn't guaranteed, he trusted the men in his immediate circle. They all had a new status's and six-figure incomes. The mentor program was on a rise and now that he had a mountain of money, he was ready to expand. B-Smoove was his personal assistant and Gavin gifted him a mega mansion located in Valley Forge, a sports car and a ridiculous salary. He wanted to keep him close. After everything they been through the past couple of months, he was still worried about his sanity.

Ms. Rhonda and Garin continued to run his daycares and Ms. Rhonda was ready to expand the business and open shop in Jersey. The school was competitive and baby mothers would kill for their babies and toddlers to be enrolled.

Life was back to normal and everyone was at peace. However, Gavin wanted a change, and he wanted to make sure his family was safe. Especially, after Ciani told him she was pregnant again. He was overjoyed with the news and since Bill's death, he was much more active with little Gavin. As far as the money, only Ciani and Bill's people knew he was beyond balling.

"Cee, I was thinking, and you never got that vacation I promised you. Let's go somewhere, anywhere pick a place!" he suggested.

"I mean, we do have the house in Colorado and I never been. We should go just to see how the house looks," she replied.

"It's beautiful! I saw it one time, but I was thinking about something grander!"

"Bae, long as I'm by your side, I don't care," she said.

She was no help and Gavin knew he would have to make the decision.

Later they snuggled in the bed and watched late night tv. He was about to cut it off when one of those heartbreaking infomercials came on with starving children. His heart was heavy, and it was hard to watch, but something wouldn't allow him to turn.

"Damn, every time I watch one of these commercials, I get mad!" he said disgusted by the elite and the lack of humanity. He gave occasionally, but he was ready to do more. "Bae, I need you to do some research. Find a few poor countries like this that we can help. I want to do more than give a donation. I want to help in a way that it can really change a village!" he explained ready to invest outside the hood.

"I'm glad you said village, because I already know how you are! Remember we can't save the world, but we must trust that God will order our footsteps and place us where we need to be! I'll check on that first thing in the morning," she responded.

"Nah, you can check it on when we get back from Colorado! Let's take the whole family and have real celebration of life. I'll ask mom to get all the family members onboard. We'll call it Gavin's Magnificent Reunion!"

"You're so full of yourself! But, I'm excited, bae."

"I got a surprise for you in that top drawer. Open it and

pull out the envelope," he instructed, and she complied. She opened the envelope and went ballistic.

"Oh my, God! The marriage license, Gavin! Thank you, Heavenly Father, my prayers have been answered. I'm so happy!" she hollered.

"Now, you officially belong to me though you always did. Wife for life!

"I know that's right cause's you want me taking half of this kingdom," she joked. But, seriously, I have something for you. She reached in her purse and pulled out a sealed letter and handed it to Gavin.

"What's this?" he asked

"You'll see," she replied, and he read the letter in silence. After Bill died and Gavin inherited the money, she wrote her own prenup and had it notarized.

"Ciani, why did you do this, sweetheart?" He was angry and touched at the same. Her requests were reasonable and minimal. She only wanted support payments and a house.

"Listen, you would be a fool if you didn't get a prenup. I knew you wouldn't get one, so I took the matter in my own hands. Don't get me wrong, I feel blessed that my man has money, but the money Bill left—you need to protect yourself. Just give that to your lawyer and I'll also make a verbal statement," she explained. Gavin had no intentions fulfilling her wishes, but he decided to have a little fun.

"You know, babe good looking out. I forgot all about protecting myself from you. You see, the spell and hold you got on me. You can never be too safe, because women change like wind, but you, more like a storm! Thanks bae!" he replied, and her facial expression turned sour, but she quickly recovered.

"You're welcome. I should pack for the trip," she replied and attempted to get out the bed.

"Where you going?" he asked and tackled her back on the bed. He kissed her while groping her vagina then prickling her supple nipples, sending plutonium vibrations throughout her entire body. "There's no need for a prenup, Cee because I'm never letting you go! You're it!" He stood up and ripped the paper to shreds. "Stop thinking about shit like that! That's your problem, Cee sometimes you think too hard. Just be happy bae! You got me!"

"Yes boss!"

For the next few months, they traveled and visited their homes in Beverly Hills and Colorado Springs. Ciani fell in love with Colorado and wanted to stay forever. However, Gavin strong desire to be close to the hood, threw that dream out the window, but Gavin compromised, and they came up with a housing resolution. Ciani suggested they stay a few months out the year at each home and Gavin agreed. She showed how he could run his business from anywhere in the world.

Currently, they were residing at the Beverly Hills home and Ciani loved the home, but she wished she could pick it up and place anywhere else. Beverly Hills wasn't her thing, but Gavin and Salas were bonding on a friendship level and Salas kept him busy. Annabella took Ciani under her wing and they built of a wonderful friendship. They went on shopping sprees and girl's trips. Annabella was pregnant too and showed Ciani how to be stress free while carrying a load. Ciani was much at peace with this pregnancy and Gavin was relived.

The Douglas's finally had peace and normalcy and Gavin had his Magnificent Revenge!

The End